MURDER
at the
QUILT
SHOW

To Lee

QIP

Quilt Inn Publishing
1995

Quilt Inn Publishing
P.O. Box 6034
Englewood, CO 80155-6034

Printed in USA
First Quilt Inn Publishing Printing: January 1995
10 9 8 7 6 5 4 3

ISBN 0-9696491-9-3

Attention Schools and Corporations:

Quilt Inn Publishing books are available at quantity discounts with bulk purchase for educational, business or sales promotional use. For information, please write to:

Michael Patten
Quilt Inn Publishing
P.O. Box 6034
Englewood, CO 80155-6034

Other Books by Aliske Webb

Twelve Golden Threads
Scrap Quilt Memories
The Quilt Inn Country Cookbook

To my Grama
Alice Meyers Staley

and to
quilters everywhere
who love a good yarn

The Cast of Characters

The Guild

Carmen Sanchez
President
Joan Dixon
Past President
Carol Ann Rafferty
Treasurer
Rosemary Campbell
Quilt Show Chair
Angela Patten
Merchant Mall Chair
LeaAnn Dent
Publicity Chair

Various members including:

Susan Patten
Gladys Brock
Annemarie Schmidt
Betty Harrison
Kay Sturm

The Merchants

Angela Patten
Grama's Quilt Shop
Roberta Walker
Scratchin' To Patch
Gerry & Marion Cooper
The Antique Attic
Horace Roundtree
Temple of Templates
Penny Prescott
Penny Cotton
Candice Moore
Candy Cane's Country
Dixie Robinson
The Quilt Peddler

The Judges

Beryl Carter
Tom Lansdowne
Audry Mills

The Town

Al Brown, Sr., Mayor
John Murphy, Security Guard
Judy Marshall, Deputy Sheriff
Charlie Waite, Security Guard
J.B. (Jeff Bob) Burnet, Sheriff
Brad Gilmour, Editor, The Banner
Luther Blaine, Photographer, The Banner

Clareville is hosting a Quilt Show.

The Quilt Show Committee has labored long and hard for months. Tasks are assigned according to ability and willingness. A myriad decisions are faced and accomplished by teams of women working for a common goal: the best darned quilt show possible! When and where to hold the show, opening hours, admission price, door prizes, raffle tickets to be sold, a raffle quilt to be created, a merchant mall to be filled, sponsors, classes and teachers to be arranged, publicity to be paid for or finagled, quilts to be finished, judges to be enlisted, volunteer "white glove ladies" to be organized.

"Do we expand this year?"

"How many quilts can we display?"

"Who will head up the committees?"

"How do we find sponsors?"

"When does the publicity have to start?"

It's a project–management exercise that would daunt NASA scientists. It's a peak experience and a team effort. A miracle entirely performed by unpaid, over–worked, volunteers. If not for an overwhelming desire to share their love of quilting, the show would never get off the launchpad, the committee table.

The eve of the show arrives. The hall is lit, the set–up workers arrive and fan out to their tasks. Like a hive of thrumming bees, they are intent upon the sweet ordeal of turning an empty chasm into a golden treasure of creativity. Row after row of frames are constructed, and quilt after quilt is draped in an orderly profusion, like giant canvases in an art gallery.

The local vendors begin arriving to set up booths in the merchant mall. These are the shopkeepers from Clareville and the smaller towns around it. Most already will be known to the committee and the quilters. They come to serve the needs of their regular customers and to be part of the excitement at the show. They fill their assigned spaces with display racks and tables carefully designed to intrigue and invite shoppers to enter, browse and take home an assortment of country quilting–related items from baskets to jewelry to pot–holders and wooden hangers. Like a community of creative artists at a Medieval Fare they fill the air with excitement, promise and cheerful chatter.

The out–of–town vendors come. They arrive from everywhere across the country, like gypsies in their chrome and steel covered wagons, bulging with wares to sell. Like travelling tinkers in caravans they bring new and useful gadgets: needles, machines, hoops, frames, cutting tools, rulers, books and patterns. Like sideshow magicians, they stage new and easy techniques to bedazzle the local customers: strip piecing magic, foundation magic, no–sew applique. And like the early Persian traders trekking along the Silk Road from China, they bear bolts of many-colored cloths: the latest Hoffman, RJR, Jinny Beyer, Momen—code names known well by the *cognoscenti*, a confusing jargon to the uninitiated.

The vendors have a long history and come from a noble tribe of merchant princes. Our pioneer grandmothers would have no trouble recognizing these camels of the modern commercial world. They are like buyers and sellers from everywhere around the world, from every time. It's an ancient dance, a celebration of the trading ritual.

The vendors come like debutantes to a Ball, all decked out, hoping someone exciting will ask them to dance. Nervous and anticipating. "Will it be a good show?" they ask one another. "Have you done this show before?" they query automatically as they introduce themselves to the vendors in booths next door to them. They are instant neighbors and comrades–in–arms, for the duration.

They share war stories.

"I was at the Williamstowne show. It was great. The quilts were terrific. I sold out of patterns by the second day."

"I did the Jonesville show. You wouldn't believe it. The Guild even provided us with a potluck lunch. And they had booth–sitters so we could take a break whenever we needed it. They really cared about us. Everyone was so friendly."

"You're lucky. I was going to do that show but I did the Thomasburg one instead. It was awful. It was poorly organized. I hardly saw any Guild members at all. It seemed like they didn't even come out to support their own show..."

"They really publicized the show well..."

"There were lots of quilts..."

"They were gorgeous..."

"There was a good selection of vendors..."

"The Guild was friendly, helpful and so well organized..."

Every mysterious factor that accumulates into the equation resulting in a successful show is analyzed and shared. No show is perfect. Everyone looks for the best combination of a myriad of variables. Like hunters, they go where the game is plentiful.

The tom–toms beat. Word travels the grapevine from vendor to vendor. Like hobos who place a secret mark on houses where a down–and–out traveller is likely to be offered a meagre meal or dry shed to sleep in, words are left in the ears of eager listeners about what towns are likely watering holes on the vendors' seasonal trek around the country. The good shows grow better, with everyone eager to attend. The bad shows grow worse, with ever–diminishing attendance and interest. Reputation is everything.

Paramount above all is the quilts. There must be lots of good quilts to look at. If the quilts are good, the public is happy. When the public is happy, they are eager to buy and the vendors are happy. When everyone is happy the Guild can be satisfied they did their exhaustive job well.

If you build it, they will come.

If you build a show that excites the imagination, dreamers will come to touch the magic. They will come to experience something greater than themselves, to be part of the creative foundation that unites us all. Because a quilt means life. It stands for warmth and abundance and beauty. It stands for all that is best in the human condition, and in the human heart.

If you build well, they will come back.

The show finally opens and the public arrives, the Guild members and the non–members, the quilters and the non–quilters. They come like honored guests to a banquet laid out specifically for their sensory delight and enjoyment. They come to be enchanted. They come to see quilts. Beautiful quilts. Exciting quilts.

Controversial quilts. *Lots* of quilts. They come with wide open eyes and wide open hearts. They come to love unconditionally everything they see. They will forgive a wayward seam, a faulty stitch, an unworthy design because they recognize in every quilt an honest try, and a reflection of their own fledgling and tentative creative steps. They celebrate the delirious colors, the painstaking detail, and the hours of commitment.

The quilters come to be educated and to share. Like turtles, they lug heavy machines, all the tools of their art, and show–and–tell projects to class. Like eager acolytes they sit at the feet of talented masters (mistresses) and absorb their wisdom, memorizing, note–taking, practising every idea to make their own quilts more exciting, challenging, glorious. Like unabashed kindergarten children, they proudly display their own less–than–perfect work, conscious that in every class is a knowing and compassionate audience.

For one day, or four days, they will eat, sleep, talk and breathe quilting, with the devotion and reverence of nuns, but without a vow of silence! Above all they came to talk and laugh. They have carved out this sacred time from lives filled with homes, families, careers, chores and the selfless caring for others. This is private time for themselves. This is communal time to be with other like–minded and obsessive quilters. This is time away, mental health time, spiritual re–freshment time, time to return to their creative roots or center with other passionate, and equally misunderstood by family and friends, women who quilt.

To quilt is heaven, to finish is divine.

To quilt is sublime.

Wise old men search for the meaning of life. They find cold comfort in their philosophies and the monastic walls of intellect.

These wise women search for the *experience of being alive*. They find connection and warmth in the communion of touch and sight and talk.

To quilt is to be alive and say, "I quilt, therefore I am."

Their quilts tell their stories. Like the outer bias–cut binding that frames and finishes a quilt, the women are contained within their quilting. Their biographies are told. Their sentiments are exposed.

By the craft, know the craftsman. By the quilt, know the passions that lie beneath.

"I am awash in rapturous hues," one exclaims.

"I am filled with nostalgic memory," whispers another.

"I am form and function," another calmly asserts.

"Look, this issue is important!" declares another angrily.

The quilters come like hopeful Goldrush prospectors with purses and dusty pokes full of gold that they will exchange for plastic carrybags full of fabric, and gadgets, and dreams. Old gold for new dreams. A fair trade without doubt. They will take away excitement and vigor. They will take away inspiration, and frustration. They arrived zealously early in the morning, and yet can't wait to return home, to start another quilt project. Their imaginations and creativity have been stirred into action. Their eyes are weary from hours of concentrated focus yet their fingers itch to handle their treasures in the familiar comfort of their own special workspace: the forge of Ulrich where they will transmute dross cotton into golden quilted sheets of wonder.

Clareville is hosting a quilt show. Passions run high. Emotions run rampant. The stage is set for mayhem.

It's just a quilt show.

Isn't it?

One

"Nothing *Gothic* ever happens in this town," Jennifer moaned miserably into her bowl of cornflakes. The morning sunlight streamed slantwise through the windows and fell on her glass of orange juice, illuminating it like a bright neon sign. She was sitting at the kitchen table in tailored pyjamas, chin on hand, distractedly twiddling her long auburn hair around two fingers of her other hand. Her mother stood at the kitchen sink filling a kettle. She glanced briefly over her shoulder and smiled. That's my baby, Angela thought affectionately. Always looking for excitement.

For most of her life, Jennifer had been a city girl, used to hustle and bustle, and adventure. She now has a love–hate relationship with the small town she's been living in for two years.

Clareville boasts an inaccurate population count posted on a greeting sign at the edge of town that declares 6,497. It should say, 'more or less, plus one cranky soul'. There is the established tree–lined downtown sometimes–brick–but–mostly–wood–frame section where time and progress seems to have touched lightly, and change is slow and superficial. The surrounding expansion of de–nuded suburban housing, strip mall businesses and light industry seems to have sprung up full–grown, like the bamboo plant that grows unnoticed underground for four years and then soars to over eighty feet almost overnight. And beyond the town is the sparse and green countryside that nourishes the town with clean air, market produce and export crops. Everywhere people move and change with the shifting sands of economics, upward mobility, age and necessity.

The sign also says, 'Founded in 1837'. This should also say, 'more or less'. The early settlers came and laboriously cleared the land, making room in the wilderness for their crops and children to thrive.

The town has continued to found itself ever since.

Angela bought the quilt shop, and the girls came to live with her shortly thereafter. Jennifer's enthusiasm blew hot and cold depending on the day. Some days, she loved the peaceful tranquility and the comfort of getting–to–know–your–neighbors that comes with a small town. Other days, she bubbled and hissed like water on a hot griddle to have stimulation and a channel for her abundant energy, and hated the everyone–knows–your–business of the townsfolk. On any day the town was the same; it was her view that changed. She was always an impetuous child and Angela had begun to wonder if she would ever outgrow her moodiness. Angela thought that at twenty–four, her eldest daughter would have started to channel her energy into one consistent direction in life.

"What's the matter? Isn't the amateur drama group *dramatic* enough for you?" asked her sister Susan sarcastically, without looking up from reading a local newspaper.

The younger daughter, Susan, at twenty–one, was the foot–on–the–floor pragmatist in the family. There was no doubt that her quiet and adaptable personality was comfortable in the small town environment. They fitted together in an amicable harmony.

"Hmphh," responded Jennifer grumpily.

"Is the Dickens pageant still not working out well?" mother

prompted her unhappy daughter.

"Yeah, it's fine," she replied with a resigned sigh, "except nobody will let their kids dress for the role of the street urchins in Fagin's gang. Everyone wants *their* precious darling to look like Little Lord Fauntleroy," Jennifer complained in annoyance.

"So? Get the grungy boys from the high school crowd to play Fagin's motley crew! They'd love the opportunity to 'dress–down' for the part!" Susan suggested, not too seriously.

"They're too big to be *urchins*," Jennifer objected.

"Artistic license," her sister shrugged, undeterred in her attempt to be practical and helpful.

"You don't understand!" Jennifer peevishly replied. "Dickens' London was a poverty– and disease–stricken era. Children were undernourished and since there weren't any child labor laws yet, they were also over–worked. They were all tiny people!"

"This is a *Christmas* pageant you're talking about, isn't it?" Susan asked pointedly. "Not *Les Miserables*!"

"I'm just after realism," Jennifer defended.

"But they are going to *sing* at least, aren't they?" Susan asked in mock concern.

At a rare loss for words, Jennifer just stuck her tongue out at her sister. Why do girls stick their tongues out as a way of punctuating and finishing losing arguments, Angela wondered to herself. It's something you never see boys doing. She tried to remember the last time her middle son, Robbie, stuck his tongue out in frustrated pique. He was probably two at the time. Now he was twenty–two, and taller than me, she smiled, thinking of him. Robbie was working on his post–graduate degree out West and rarely was able to come home for visits. Angela missed her thoughtful and good–natured young man. He's taller than his father even, she realized sadly. Jack had died over ten years ago and never knew how tall and strong his three children would grow up to be.

The whistling of the kettle broke her reverie, and as she tuned back in to the continuing dialogue, she heard Susan speaking.

"Sounds to me like what you want to do is a cross between Dickens and a television expose," Susan said finally as she folded the newspaper, stood up to leave and picked up her breakfast dishes. She walked to the sink and filled them with water.

"Well, at least that would bring some *excitement* to town! Look! The biggest news in The Banner is the Quilt Show your Guild is holding!" Jennifer declared picking up the paper and holding it out accusingly toward her mother.

"Not fair," Susan admonished. "You know the show is a big deal this year. It's the Fifteenth Biannual Show for the Guild, and Mayor Brown just declared a Quilting Week for the town as a way of supporting it!"

"Yeah, yeah," Jennifer waved off the explanation. "No offence, Mom. I know you are going to have a booth at the show and everything, but how dull can a town get when its big news is a quilt show, for heaven's sake! I want to make the pageant something to grab everyone's attention!"

"It's only the middle of September," mother soothed, ignoring the back–handed insult. "I'm sure you'll sort it all out before the time comes. You know the saying, 'It'll be alright on the night.' Which reminds me. Tonight! Don't forget I have a Guild meeting. It's the last official meeting of all the committees before the show opens. So, I'll probably be late."

"We'll leave the light on," Susan smiled as she kissed her mother's cheek on her way out the door.

Angela sat down with her favorite mug and made sure the hot teapot was under a quilted teacozy. While waiting for the tea to 'steep', she picked up the newspaper. On the front page was a picture of Mayor 'Uncle Al' Brown, and Carmen Sanchez, the President of the Clareville Quilt Guild. In the two years that Angela had owned the quilt shop, she had become good friends with Carmen, who was definitely not the best quilter in the world, but who loved quilting and quilters. She came from a family of eight brothers so she was overjoyed at finding 'sisters' in the Guild. She was friendly and kind, and an efficient president of the club.

The newspaper photo showed them shaking hands as he presented her with the declaration certificate for Quilting Week. It was a good omen, she thought, that the town was getting behind the Guild, or at least was going to be more aware of the upcoming show. It was all part of a campaign that Angela had helped initiate two years ago to revitalize the town, especially the old town square. Developers, headed by the Mayor's son, AJ, had proposed tearing it down to build a modern shopping mall.

After a long struggle, the townsfolk had come together and agreed to restore the downtown area instead, and to start cultural activities that would draw more people, and dollars, into the town. The shopfronts around the square, including her own Grama's Quilt

Shop, had been renovated into a trendy and attractive heritage shopping 'center'. The original Federal–style row of streetfront businesses had been repaired and repainted in reproduction colors to simulate the authentic ones. Coordinated signage had been created to complement the look. An old grey stone historic coach house had been turned into a museum and restaurant, The Stone House Inn. Even the townhall had been given a new coat of official off–white paint. The project had been successful already and more businesses had opened along the sidestreets that accessed the square. It was a pleasant place to spend a day or evening shopping, eating or exploring.

In the preserved tree–lined park in the middle of the square, there were Sunday concerts in the bandshell, country markets every month on Saturdays, and Jennifer's Christmas pageant.

And now the town was having a big quilt show.

Angela smiled at the photo. As Susan said, this year is special. A thirty year celebration of the Guild and its Fifteenth Biannual Quilt Show. Bigger than any show they had ever put on before. It would be four days long with a conference running in conjunction to it. There were several well–known teachers invited to give classes.

Publicity for the show had started months ago. LeaAnn Dent and the other members of her publicity committee, had contacted everyone they could think of to promote the show. She had been in touch with women's organizations, senior citizen's groups, and all the other guilds within a three hundred mile radius, and invited them to attend. Several guilds were organizing bus tours to bring their quilters to the show, and the town, for the day.

The Guild would have over 200 quilts to display. And for the first time, it would be a juried show, with nationally–accredited judges coming to decide on the prize–winners. There was prize money to be won in several categories, which had attracted entries from quilters all across the region. Even one of the travelling 'Hoffman Challenge' displays had been arranged. Hoffman is a cotton fabric manufacturer who every year challenges quilters to make wall quilts and quilted dolls using a specially chosen fabric from their line. The winning entries then go on tour to quilt shows across the country. They are in high demand, add a certain lustre to any show, and the exhibit is hard to obtain.

This year the quilt show introduced an antique auction with items donated by many leading citizens, as part of this year's theme for the show, 'Pieces of the Past'. The guild had chosen the theme because it wanted to connect quilting as a traditional folk art, and craft, to today's modern world, to bring quilting out of the closet of memories into the livingrooms of tomorrow. With all these special attractions the Clareville Quilt Show was sure to appeal to quilters and quilt lovers who might travel from a great distance. It could mean new members, and extra funds in the treasury for their charity projects, and attention for the town. It was going to be an important show.

"I hope we haven't bitten off more than we can chew," Angela said out loud.

Jennifer had leaned back in her chair and was watching her mother. Being the owner of the local quilt shop, Angela had volunteered to organize the Merchant Mall for the show and her daughters had seen the project grow from the ground up. There were almost twenty businesses coming to be part of the show, to sell everything from fabric, patterns and notions, to quilting frames, country decorations and clothing.

"You're worrying again," Jennifer admonished affectionately and waggled her finger at Angela.

Why do all daughters think their mothers are worry–warts? Perhaps because they are. Or perhaps because when you're twenty–four you're still invincible, and think everyone else is too.

Angela thought to herself, I don't know everything yet. I'm not young enough...

"You guys have been working on this project for over a year now. Don't worry. I'm sure you've thought of everything by now. And what you haven't covered, you'll handle as it happens." Although Jennifer was a tempestuous young woman, she was the child that Angela could always count on for optimistic and enthusiastic support when her spirits were flagging.

"I know," Angela nodded. "It just seems that this year is so important. A lot more people will be paying attention to what we do than before. We don't want to make a mistake."

"It'll be alright on the night, remember," Jennifer quoted back to her mother.

"Hoisted on my own petard. Again!" Angela chuckled, hearing her own words repeated back to her.

Jennifer got up to leave and patted her mom's shoulder. "Gotta go," she said, heading for the bathroom. "Having dinner with AJ tonight, so I may be a little late myself," she called over her shoulder.

"You don't know what worrying is all about", Angela said softly under her breath to the empty room. "Until you have daughters who date."

Jennifer had been dating AJ off–and–on for almost two years now. Son of the mayor and a successful young businessman, AJ was a decent sort of fellow. Although originally an instigator of the tear–down–the–square consortium, he had come around completely and was fully supportive of the preservation project. This was fuelled partly by the fact that he was now landlord to several thriving businesses in the downtown area, and partly by his unabashed interest in Jennifer. But at twenty–four, Jennifer had decided she was not ready to settle down yet. She was still in the process of 'finding herself'.

Grama used to laugh at that expression. "What is this 'find yourself'?" she would say. "And why do young people have to go somewhere else to do it? They come from here and go there. And the others are from there and come here. Why don't they all stay put!"

In the silence that was left after the girls had departed, Angela poured her tea and sat drinking it peacefully in the morning sunshine, thinking about the busy day she had ahead before the Guild meeting.

Two

The Clareville Quilt Guild gets together every second Tuesday evening of the month at seven o'clock. The eighty members, and occasional guests–cum–new–recruits, meet downtown in the Jonathan Cooper-Smythe church hall on Clifford Street. 'Doc' Smythe had spearheaded the fund-raising to build the hall in the Fifties and therefore received the honor of having it named after him. It is the same hall that the Guild has met in for the last thirty years. The Guild has outlasted three ministers. The shepherds come and go, the flock stays.

Inside the hall, the cinder–block walls have been painted many times. The present pale yellow color is punctuated in spots with the previous pale green color, where masking tape has pulled off chunks of paint disclosing the archeological layering beneath. Every once in a while someone in the congregation suggests painting the hall again, debate surfaces momentarily, funds are examined, and ultimately colorful travel posters or signs are found to cover any new offending bald spots, and the pale yellow continues to glow softly for another year.

Most of the time the hall is empty except for an assortment of curved wooden–seat and metal–frame chairs along with eight–foot wood tables that are scarred, carved, gouged and cigarette–burned with casual and careless use. It's a Japanese concept of interior design function—the room becomes whatever you bring into it. Bring in crepe paper streamers, cookies on paper plates and toys and it becomes a creche. Introduce war vets, beer and poker chips and the same space becomes a smokey bear den. Bring in fabric and quilters and it becomes a beehive.

To one side at the back of the hall is a kitchen where refreshments are prepared and served over a the half–height dividing wall. Inside there are mismatched, painted wooden cupboards and counters, a chipped white refrigerator with rounded edges reminiscent of a 1952 Buick that hint at its unknown vintage, an avocado green stove that was donated by a home–renovating family in 1982, and an incongruously modern, but useful, microwave. The thirty–cup dented aluminum percolator has seen better days but still brews a mean, if slightly metallic, cup of coffee. Donated appliances, all gratefully employed.

So, the hall is old and the furniture is old. And some of the faces are old. But the enthusiasm is forever new and no one much notices the surroundings unless the heat goes off, or one of the fluorescent lights starts to flicker annoyingly.

Quilters know that when life gives you scraps, make quilts.

What's important after all? To the quilters it is the opportunity to get together once a month to talk about quilting, to share their experiences, to learn new techniques, to show off and to applaud others. And to have a hoot an' a holler while they do so. This is not a quiet group.

This is not a sedate group of timid old ladies.

These are working women from all social classes, and women with families, and retired women. They are busy and passionate and humorous. They are kind and helpful and nurturing. In other words, they exhibit all the fine qualities that their quilts do. By the creation, know the creator. By the quilt, know the quilter.

They are also opinionated and speak up, at least here within the safe group. They are women of every political faction and religion. Yet they all pay homage to the vitality of the feminine creative spirit.

They are cranky and don't always like each other. If it weren't for quilting, for most of them, their paths might never have crossed.

They are friends. They are rivals, and they all love quilting.

Angela closed and locked the front doors of her shop. She rang out the till, tidied up the cutting table and returned wyward bolts of fabric to their proper shelves. It was a familiar routine that she performed almost in a trance. Like a rhythmic meditation, the order and pattern of her movements was a comforting end to the day. It provided her with a few moments of closure and reverie. Her thoughts inevitably flowed to memories of 'Grama', Jack's mother, who had died four years ago. She had been Angela's spiritual mentor, in quilting, and in life. The long, narrow shop was named in her honor. It was a place Grama would have felt at home in.

Her ritual completed, Angela moved to the back of the shop and reached out to turn off the light switch. She took one last look around and said softly, "Goodnight Grama," as she did every night, and then climbed the stairs to her apartment above to get ready for the guild meeting.

Half an hour later she walked briskly across the town square, and down several short sidestreets to the church hall. Because she had to close her shop, the meeting had already started when Angela arrived. Carmen had opened the meeting, made her comments and was calling on the various committee chairwomen to give their latest official reports.

The Guild Treasurer, Carol Ann Rafferty, had already submitted her report, as Angela sidled into a seat in the back. Good thing, she sighed to herself. Carol Ann had been Treasurer for many years. It's often a job nobody else wants. It's dull and tedious and it fit her to a 'T'. Naturally enough, Carol Ann was also an immaculate quilter who made incredibly tiny miniature quilts. Like ships in bottles, the how–did–she–do–it intrigued anyone who saw her work. But, like listening to her detailed and excting financial report, no one really wanted to listen to the answer.

Rosemary Campbell, as Quilt Show Committee Chairwoman, was the overall organizer for the show. Although she had been on several committees in past years, this was her first year as Chair and she had worked overtime ensuring that every last detail was looked after. The stress was starting to show. Although she smiled constantly, there was a frown embedded in her brow. As the pressure mounted nearer the show date, she was more distracted and often lost her focus in the middle of a sentence. She's on overload, Angela thought sympathetically.

LeaAnn was a good choice for the publicity committee. She was young, bright and outgoing and wouldn't take 'no' for an answer. You can never have enough publicity, Angela said to herself. Too often guilds just run a couple of ads, sit back thinking that's all they have to do, and then wonder why no one turns up. LeaAnn had brought in some creative new ideas about how the Guild could publicize the show, and she had been strong enough to convince the status quo–seekers to try something different.

Angela gave her own report on the merchant mall that would be part of the show. Including her own booth, she had eighteen booths rented for a reasonable fee with what she thought was a n interesting mixture of products and services for quilters. "Just be sure there is lots of fabric for quilters to see", was the advice she had been given when she volunteered for the job.

With the business portion of the agenda attended to, Annemarie Schmidt took over the evening's program. She had arranged for an actress who specialized in re–enactment scenarios to come and perform for them. 'Lavinia' was the name of the character that the actress portrayed. She was a lively and humorous country woman who sat at a spinning wheel and dished out a running commentary on her life and times in an earthy and honest fashion. She had cleverly adapted her talk to incorporate comments about the quilt that she would ultimately make from the thread she was spinning, and that really tickled the guild members. For the whole hour she had the audience giggling and guffawing, and in tears. A rousing and spontaneous standing ovation broke out at the end of the presentation.

Annemarie presented 'Lavinia'–Sue with a special small quilted wall hanging that had been prepared for her in advance, along with an envelope containing her fee. Everyone complimented Annemarie on the wonderful job she was doing as program chairwoman, bringing in interesting and innovative speakers to the meetings.

The last item on the agenda was always 'bring–and–brag'. Or 'drag–and–brag' as some referred to it. This is the time when anyone who wishes to has the opportunity to show off their latest project. Many of the quilts that would appear in the upcoming Quilt Show had been pre–viewed at these monthly sessions as works–in–progress. Moved by the ephemeral hands of creativity, each quilter decides on her own when her time has come, when it was time to deliver and show her baby. It need not even be finished. It could be merely a quilt top, finally pieced and ready for quilting. It could even be various completed blocks, appliqued and ready for setting into a top. It could be an old quilt, a treasure found, or saved from demolition. Or slides of a recent trip. Or any other source of inspiration that moved the quilter, and was deemed worthy of sharing.

Each exhibiting quilter momentarily takes center stage at the front of the room and describes her trophy. For many of these women, it is the only time in their lives they would stand in front of so large an audience. The new members would come shyly, but proudly and with courage because they already knew from the months of enviously watching others, that every effort would be applauded, every inspiration would be acknowledged, and that eloquence was unnecessary when the quilt spoke for you.

The highlight for tonight's show–and–tell was the completion of the raffle quilt. Every year the Guild as a group makes a quilt to be raffled off to raise funds. The funds are used to buy fabric and batting to make comfort quilts for the children's wards of hospitals throughout the state. The raffle quilt committee would decide on the design, buy the fabric and plan the quilt. The membership at large was invited to help construct it, from piecing blocks to doing the elaborate hand quilting. So everyone had seen the quilt progress over the past few months.

This year's quilt was a pieced quilt, a 'sampler' that incorporated twenty traditional block designs and was heavily hand-quilted. It was made of calicoes and stripes in old–fashioned blue-beige-brown-maroon hues to give it an antique look, in keeping with their show theme, 'Pieces of the Past'. It was an impressive quilt and everyone was proud of the results.

The members had been selling tickets for several weeks. More tickets would be sold at the show, and the drawing would be at four o'clock on Sunday, the last day of the show. In the meantime, for the next four weeks, the quilt would be displayed in the Town Hall lobby to publicize the show. The raffle quilt was always one of the best sources of revenue for the guild.

Angela always found these show–and–tell sessions to be uplifting. She smiled happily as the meeting adjourned on the upbeat note, for refreshments and free–for–all chatter.

Balancing her notepad, a cup of tea and a doughnut, Angela made her way toward Betty Harrison, who was in charge of the quilt hanging crew for the show. These two women would be the busiest organizers on the day of the set up, the day before the show opened. Angela would be overseeing all the vendors moving in their displays and goods. Betty would be supervising the crews of volunteers who would be hanging the many quilts. Everyone would be accessing the same entrance doors and working in the same hall, at the same time. It was important that they work cooperatively or 'set–up' could become a shambles of chaos. So far they had been getting along fine, jokingly calling themselves 'The A Team', while everyone else was the 'Z' team, meaning they could catch some 'z's while the 'real work' was being done. Conversely, once the show was constructed, Angela and Betty could sit back, relax somewhat and enjoy themselves. At least until Sunday afternoon when the 'tear–down' would begin.

As Angela approached, she heard the tail end of the conversation Betty was having with several Guild members.

"You know the quilts all have to be submitted to the committee at least one week before the show!" Betty was chastising someone, who simply walked away from her without saying anything. Betty was left shaking her head in annoyance.

"What's wrong?" Angela asked, putting down her tea and notepad and taking a bite of the doughnut.

"Gladys," Betty replied as if that was enough of an explanation in itself.

Angela nodded. The two women had a polite but distinct dislike for each other at the best of times. Although they were both expert quilters, their personalities clashed like fire and ice, Tom and Jerry, Luke Skywalker and Darth Vader, oil and water, or any other adversarial opposite you can name. Gladys Brock was as calm and soft–spoken as Betty Harrison was effusive and emotional. Their natural tendencies seemed to become magnified and even more strongly entrenched when face to face with their opposite.

As head of the quilt hanging crew Betty had a tremendous responsibility to ensure not only the security of the quilts against loss or damage, but also the final attractive layout of the show. She was happy to be in control of such an important project and was probably throwing her weight around. And Gladys was stubborn enough not to pay her any attention.

"She says she won't be delivering her quilt to the show until the day of set–up. She knows we have to look at all the quilts beforehand. So we know where to hang them! I've half a mind to hang her quilt in the washroom if she doesn't see fit to cooperate!" Betty was incensed at the wrinkle in her otherwise orderly plan.

"At least everyone would be sure to see it there," someone joked lightly.

"I'll talk to her," Angela offered and made a mental note to find the recalcitrant quilter sometime during the evening.

In the meantime she spoke casually with several members of the Guild. As the local shopowner, Angela was frequently looked to for technical advice, or for sourcing of products someone needed. It was a role she enjoyed. Having been in the psychological counselling profession for twenty years prior to opening the quilt store, Angela was comfortable and practised at prompting and promoting the quilters to find their own answers within themselves, rather than simply following the tried–and–true 'rules'. She felt that it was important that the whole process of making a quilt be an empowering and creative experience for the women in her group. In effect, that made her a gifted teacher, although she would never have defined herself as such.

It was an hour later when Angela spotted Gladys again and decided to approach her on the subject of the quilt.

"You're looking tired, " Angela commented gently as she sat down beside her friend at one of the long wooden tables. There were dark circles under Gladys' eyes and she was looking unusually subdued. "Been burning the candle at both ends again quilting?" she joked.

Gladys smiled wanly and nodded. Everyone in the Guild knew that Gladys had quit her job a month ago. After seven apparently contented years as a paralegal for a local law firm, her sudden decision to resign was a surprise. She never gave a satisfactory reason for leaving and had spent her unoccupied day times feverishly working on her quilting. Whenever anyone asked, she would simply say, "It's just something I have to do." Eventually everyone stopped asking.

"I guess so," she said quietly, as if the very effort of speaking was a tremendous burden on her strength. "I bet you've come to nag me about my quilt, too, haven't you?" Gladys said warily, going straight to the point and being disarmingly straightforward.

"Not really," Angela lied tactfully. "I thought you weren't looking well and I was concerned that you're not overworking yourself. You've lost weight over the summer. Are you OK?"

Angela noticed that Gladys' normally well-tailored clothes seemed to hang on her in a slightly dishevelled manner.

Gladys nodded yes. "Just an early Christmas diet." She shrugged off any further enquiries.

"Since you mentioned it, will you have any trouble finishing your quilt in time for the Show? Is there anything I can do to help?" Angela prompted. A lot of Guild members were struggling with their last minute dash to finish a project for the show. Even though quilters love to quilt, they procrastinate terribly. Angela knew all too well. She had her own set of unfinished projects still waiting for the time and inspiration to complete. Unfortunately, it was hard to finish the existing projects when there was always a new and exciting one to start.

"Not really, but thanks. I suppose I should say, 'Yes, I won't be able to finish it early', and that way everyone will leave me alone," she said honestly, apparently weary of answering questions. "Truth is, I want to keep it until just before the show opens before anyone sees it." Gladys paused.

It seemed obvious that she was expecting Angela to question why. But sensing this, Angela decided not to push, feeling that if she did Gladys wouldn't then tell her anyway. Gladys had become uncharacteristically irascible lately.

The two women sat quietly for several minutes watching the other quilters milling around the room. Gladys finally spoke again.

"In fact," she said slowly, "this is a quilt I've been thinking about making for a long, long time. It's something different and I'm not sure how some people will... react to it," she said carefully.

"I can understand that," Angela consoled her, wondering what the quilt would look like. Gladys was an expert quilter and anything she decided to do would undoubtedly be spectacular, as always. This lack of confidence wasn't like Gladys at all. She must really be tired, Angela thought gently, studying the other woman's face. She's wearing a lot more make–up than usual, she noticed.

"I guess there will be a story to tell about it," Gladys continued. "It's something new. But it's something old, too, of course," she added quickly, "in keeping with the theme."

"We'll all look forward to seeing it," Angela said sincerely. She patted Gladys' shoulder as she rose to leave.

She could honestly say to Betty that she had spoken to Gladys about the matter. In the end, like all quilters, she would do exactly as she needed and wanted to do. She would fulfil her obligation to produce the quilt, but on her own terms. That's all anyone had the right to ask.

Three

The day before the Quilt Show finally arrived. Wednesday dawned mild and drizzly. Low clouds hung over the foggy ground, blending grey–on–grey tones that drooped like wet silk over the town. The sky hung heavily like a monotonously hand-painted tapestry over the old buildings around the town square. Soft misty rain fell like a painful sigh, waterfalling from the high tree tops to the low bushes to the soggy grass below. It was a day of heavy sighs.

Angela sighed into her coffee cup as she pondered the weather. She was sitting on a cushion in the bay window of her apartment, overlooking the square. The apartment was conveniently located right over her shop. Outside wet tires made popping noises like rice cereal as cars drove by on the soggy streets below.

Angela sighed again as she thought about the effect of the weather on the quilt show's attendance. Some people would say the *bad* weather will keep everyone indoors at home and not at the show. Others would say that *good* weather means everyone will be outside and busy with other activities. The positive spin doctors would say that bad weather gives people a reason to find something interesting to do indoors for the day and therefore they *will* come and spend it at the show. They would also say that good weather means people will be happier and more outgoing and will be looking for exciting things to do, so they *will* come to the show. In the end, everything gets blamed on the weather. It doesn't seem to matter, Angela decided. Weather never stopped anyone from doing something they really want to do.

"Cheer up!" Susan smiled as she loaded a new film into her camera. "It's supposed to clear up early and be sunny all weekend."

Angela sighed again and nodded.

Jennifer was downstairs loading the last boxes into the van. Susan and Angela would drive to the show together. Jennifer would join them in the afternoon when the girls would set up Angela's booth, as she supervised the other vendors moving in. Jennifer would then be heading to the airport, to catch a shuttle. She was attending a conference in St. Louis for the weekend.

The Guild has rented the modern Alice M. Clare Community Center for the show. Ironically, it was named for the wife of the town's founding father. She had been a suffragist before there was a word for it. In the rough and tumble settlement times, she was a whiskey–drinking, poker–playing, shotgun–toting woman who could hold her own against any man. When her middle–aged philandering husband was shot, literally by a jealous husband, her only comment was, "It's lucky I didn't get to him first. There wouldn't have been enough pieces of him left to pray over." She survived him by twenty–five years, and lived long enough to see the town take a permanent toehold on the land, and to exchange her frontier audacity for salon manners. She built the town's first orphanage which continued in operation until the late 1930's. Rough packages sometimes disguise soft interiors. A pariah in her own time, honored generations later.

The Community Center is a sedate purpose–built red–brick

and concrete building in a suburban complex with an arena and sports facility, and a library next door. It's only a half a mile from the new shopping mall, so everyone hopes the convenient parking and easy accessibility will promote public interest in the Quilt Show. There is also a modern and reasonably–priced hotel chain two blocks away for the out–of–town conference attendees and vendors to stay at. This is also where the quilting classes will be held.

At 7:30 in the morning Carol Ann Rafferty was the first to arrive and was greeted at the door by John Murphy, the overnight security guard who would soon be going off shift. He unlocked the double doors at the entrance foyer and greeted her cheerfully.

"Mornin', m'am. You're the first here. When do you need all the loading doors opened?" he asked.

"Soon as possible, John," she replied. "We have a commercial design company hired to provide staging, and more vendors this year, so there will be a lot of people coming and going today as we set up. The rest of the committee should be here any minute."

"I don't normally open up the hall until eight o'clock but I guess we can leave the front door open now for the rest of your committee," he said, as he secured the emergency pressure bars into the unlocked position. He walked with her to the banquet hall. "I'll get the lights for you."

"Thanks," she replied with a warm smile.

The lights came on and flooded the cavernous room with a glare. Unlike the church hall, it was a well–used facility with a reliable air conditioning system, clean new wallpaper and carpets that muffled sounds—so unlike the harsh linoleum floor in the

Cooper–Smythe church hall. The banquet hall was a modern ballroom that could be segmented into three separate rooms by retractable walls. The quilt show would occupy all three spaces.

Carol Ann shook her head and whistled softly at the bright void.

"We have a long way to go," she sighed at the thought of the day ahead.

"Hi!" called a voice behind her. Susan came in lugging a camera case and two bulging carrybags. Her mother had dropped her at the front doors, out of the rain, and driven around back to park near the loading docks. "I hope we can get coffee this morning," she said, off–loading the equipment and pulling a camera from its bag.

Susan had caught the family quilting bug from her grandmother. She was also a member of the Guild, and had been elected Guild historian. As an amateur photographer, she enjoyed taking photographs of all the Guild activities and often helped the other members to take photos of their quilts.

"Yeah, it'll be here soon. Someone's bringing muffins, too," Carol Ann replied.

"Do me a favor," Susan said. "Go stand in the middle of the room. I want to take a picture now while it's empty. I'm going to document the whole show. Brad said he might use a couple of pictures in a story for The Banner, but the rest will be for the Guild archives. I thought it would be interesting to have a sort of stop–action series of shots every half hour through the day to see how the show looks as it is set up."

Brad Gilmour is the editor of the local newspaper. He would

be sending his one and only peripatetic reporter, Luther, to cover the opening of the quilt show.

"Great idea," Carol Ann replied and walked to the center of the space and struck a pose. "How's this?" she asked as she stood on one foot with her arms and leg stretched out wide.

"Great! Now just hold it, and smile," Susan said and popped the photo just as a banging started on the back doors to the hall.

"Early birds," Susan said.

"Early birds and eager beavers," Carol Ann replied.

They went and opened the hall doors and were greeted by four laughing committee members, bearing sacks and boxes, and puffing with exertion and merriment.

"If Kay tells one more joke, I'm going to pee my pants," Lydia chuckled.

Kay ignored the threat. Despite themselves, everyone stopped to listen as she spoke.

"You know, years ago, there was a quilter from Clareville who had been working on a 'Cathedral Windows' quilt. She took a trip to Europe to visit all the legendary churches and cathedrals there. Looking for inspiration and design ideas, you know.

"Anyway, she goes into Wells Cathedral in England and sees this sign at the back of the nave hanging over the telephone and it says, 'Talk directly to God: one thousand pounds'. 'That's weird', she says to herself, and then carries on.

"Next stop she's in Chartres Cathedral in France and she sees another sign at the back, hanging over the telephone and it says, 'Talk directly to God: ten thousand francs'.

"Well, after that, she started to see these signs everywhere she went, Italy, Greece, everywhere! Eventually she ends up back home and the following Sunday she goes to church. After the service, she approached her minister and told him about the signs. 'Talk to God: thousands of dollars', she told him. He calmly replied, 'I guess you've never noticed it but we have one of those telephones here in the church'. 'No way,' she says. 'Yes, indeed. Come and I'll show you,' he tells her and leads her to the back of the church, and sure enough, there is a telephone with a tiny little sign that says, 'Talk directly to God: twenty-five cents'. 'Wait a minute,' she says, 'how come in all those Cathedrals it was a thousand dollars, or ten thousand francs or whatever and here it's just twenty-five cents?'

"The minister smiled and shrugged as he said, 'Well, of course, from here it's a local call!'"

The women all groaned and laughed in spite of themselves. Even John joined in the merriment.

"You ladies sure are bright–eyed and bushy–tailed this morning!" John commented. He had followed them into the room from the back hallway where he met the other women as he was unlocking the loading dock doors that accessed the banquet room through the service hallway.

"All the loading doors are open," he said to Carol Ann as he also secured the hall doors into the unlocked position. "If you need anything else, I'm off duty at eight o'clock. Just check at the office. Charlie can help you. He's on duty through the weekend from eight to five."

"Thanks. We'll take it from here," she replied.

Within the first half hour, the rest of the committee members arrived, along with several conscripted husbands in jeans and overalls. Vans and cars filled with more boxes and sacks of quilts arrived and were unloaded. Betty, along with Angela, was stationed at the back exit doors and checked off the quilt bags as they arrived. Two husbands with a copy of the detailed floorplan and a surveyor's tape measured off a grid on the carpet and temporarily marked all the pre–assigned display areas with masking tape.

At 8:30 the commercial display company arrived. They had been hired to provide all the pipe–and–drape framing for the quilts to be hung on, and to divide off each of the vendors' spaces. It would take them most of the morning to erect the framework maze that creates all the corridors and viewing areas for the displays. Everyone agreed that the professional draping would give this show a distinctly classier look than in previous years.

Shortly before noon, as soon as the display company had completed the center of the hall, the committee swarmed like impatient wasps into the maze and started to lay out the bags of quilts. The juried show was an open competition and as a result there had been quilts submitted by members from guilds all across the region. Each quilt that was entered in the show had to be sent in its own marked bag.

The bags were of every size, shape and description. Some were purpose–sewn for the special quilt it contained. Others were nothing more than an old pillowcase. Many were stitched from remnants of gaudy or garish fabric that had no other use, and belied the beautiful quilts inside. Each bag had previously been numbered by the committee and was placed in front of the spot where it would hang according to the numbered floorplan. It would take a dozen people, working in groups of three, several hours to hang all the quilts.

With fortunate timing, the last of the pipe–and–drape framing around the perimeter of the hall, where the merchants' booths would be located, had been erected just as the first early vendor arrived to set up. They would be allowed all afternoon, until early evening, if necessary, to set up their booths.

By 2:00 there was a traffic jam at the loading docks. Inevitably someone selfishly parked their van right in front of the doors which meant everyone else had to work around them. Repeated requests by the committee to be considerate of others went unheeded as the vans piled up near the doors. It made it almost impossible for the orderly move in Angela had planned. There were minor skirmishes, and barely disguised irritable exchanges in the to– and fro–ing of handcarts.

As Merchant Mall organizer Angela and her committee were now stationed at the back doors that accessed the hallway leading to the loading docks, registering vendors as they arrived. Each vendor was handed a registration package that contained their official nametags, show programs and information sheets. No one would be allowed into the hall without proper identification nametags. The committee sorted out minor emergencies and tried to accommodate everyone. As always, there were last minute requests for extra tables, or chairs, or electrical hook-ups.

Angela approached the security guard who was on duty at the

back doors. "Charlie, can't you do anything about this mess?" she asked as handcarts and people bearing boxes pushed past her.

"Not really. I can only look after security inside the building, Mrs. Patten. It's going to be worse on the take–down," he gloomily predicted, "when everyone is in a hurry to go home and wanting to leave at the same time."

"Looks like chaos here!" said Gladys Brock, smiling as she walked in through the back doors bearing a quilt sack.

"Oh, hello Gladys!" Angela greeted her warmly. She hadn't seen her since their last Guild meeting. Gladys looked less haggard and more like her old self. "You look great today! And I see you finally brought your quilt for us to see. You think it's bad out here, wait until you see the hall. Rosemary is swamped. She'll be glad you're here though." Angela waved her away as she was called on to settle a dispute.

Gladys made her way to the main hall through the back doors that connected to the service access hallway. She chuckled as she entered the room and saw the maelstrom of activity.

"Busy, busy, busy," she hummed to herself. "I'm glad it's not my problem anymore," she said under her breath as she approached Rosemary.

The two women hugged warmly and the Quilt Show chairwoman shook her head saying, "You never told me it would be so much work! I wish you hadn't picked this year to step down. You should be doing this, not me!" she laughed.

"Six shows in twelve years is enough for me," Gladys replied cheerfully. "I had to let someone else have all the fun! Where do you want this?" She jiggled the bag in her arms.

"Oh, your quilt! Great! Let's see." Rosemary flipped through her papers. "It is number 103, second aisle, near the front."

"I'll find it," Gladys assured her and went forward into the hubbub. Gladys dropped her quilt at its designated spot and went on to help one of the crews hang quilts in the rest of the show. Three hours later, on her way out, she passed by the alcove where her quilt had been hung by one of the other crews. She smiled at it, pleased with herself.

"Not a bad job," she said to herself as she stood looking at it. She remained there for a long time remembering the inspiration she had for making the quilt, and wondering what people would think of it. In a sense, she didn't care what anyone thought anymore. She had made the quilt for herself, because it was something she wanted to say. "Every quilt tells a story," she commented to no one in particular, and then made her way to the back doors again.

On the way, she turned the corner at the end of an aisle of quilts and came upon Candice Moore, owner of "Candy Cane's Country" and a vendor at the show, whose back was to her. It was a workday for all the vendors, so Candice was wearing bluejeans and a torn sweatshirt. Her usually flamboyant red hair was pushed under a baseball cap. Her unadorned appearance didn't seem to stop Candice from flirting. She was talking animatedly to a tall, bearded man in a jacket and tie, standing very close to him, and touching his arm as she spoke. Everyone else was dressed in work clothes and jeans so he didn't look like he belonged to the show. He was looking uncomfortable and ill at ease.

Gladys heard Candice say, "We should go for a coffee and talk about..." but the end was cut off as someone pushing a heavily–loaded handcart called out, "Coming through!" She stepped aside to let him pass and by the time the aisle was clear, the man had gone.

Gladys smiled at Candice as she walked by. "Caught you up to something else," she muttered to herself. In return, as if reading her mind, Candice pushed her glasses up on her nose and gave Gladys a stern mind–your–business look, staring at her without speaking as Gladys passed on by.

Outside, the day had cleared and the bright Fall sun was low in the sky as Gladys left the community center. She waved at Angela as she went out the back door and disappeared into the long shadows of early evening.

On the other side of the hall, the quilt hanging crew was beginning to disperse. Betty thanked them all for their hard work and reminded them to return on Sunday evening at five o'clock sharp for the take–down, when the whole show would be dismantled, in the reverse order as today's set–up.

"Did you finally see Gladys Brock's quilt?" someone asked.

"Yes! I think it's gorgeous!" Kay Sturm enthused. "I bet you it will win top prize!"

"Don't let Betty hear you say that," a third voice warned.

"It's not about who wins or loses," Annemarie added. "They are both talented quilters. Who cares about what the judges say!"

The last remark was said a little too loudly. Someone poked the speaker and nodded in the direction of the neatly dressed man now standing near them, talking to one of the other committee members.

"Careful. That's one of the judges!" someone warned.

"Isn't that Tom Lansdowne?" Kay asked. A nod answered the question. "I hear he's a good teacher. I'm taking his class on historical quilts on Saturday."

With that, the group broke up and returned to packing up to leave.

At 5:30 the quilt–hanging crew stopped near the front door as it was leaving to pose and wave at Susan in her "crow's nest" position atop the ladder, as she took her half–hourly photo. A few yards away, behind a drape, the camera also caught Betty standing in front of Gladys' quilt, looking forlornly at the finally–completed masterpiece.

It was, after all, a magnificent quilt. After studying the quilt for several minutes, Betty was overcome with emotion and suddenly left the hall through the back door to the corridor where she could exit out the side of the building. She didn't want to be seen crying.

Quilting is sometimes a lonely obsession. It's like writing a book. You sit in a quiet solitary room, bidding the friendly muses to come, working away, working away, with a passion to complete the creation, and with a nagging in the back of your head that says, "Will anybody ever see my work? Will anybody like it?"

Certainly Gladys needn't have worried. Several people had already taken notice of her quilt.

She had stopped on the way home to pick up groceries and she had just arrived home and was unpacking bags when the telephone rang.

"Hello," she answered, and listened to the agitated voice on the other end. "Well, I agree," she said, and listened some more. "Fine. I'll see you then. We'll have a cup of tea and talk about it." She hung up the phone. Someone already wanted to talk to her about the quilt. She smiled with satisfaction as she finished unpacking her groceries.

As she intended, every half hour during the day, Susan climbed a tall ladder she left standing in the front corner of the hall in order to take a bird's–eye shot as the show began to take shape throughout the day. At first the room was empty. Then a skeleton of grey metal pipes began to take shape. Blue drapes were added that obstructed some of the view. Sporadically, the vendor's booths appeared out of nowhere. The antiques in the auction area sprouted magically. Finally all the quilts were hung and except for the occasional worker left in the hall, the show was ready for inspection.

At 7:00, just before the judges were supposed to arrive, she made a tour of the quilt show and photographed a random sample of the quilts, along with the antiques on display in the auction area. The last photo Susan took was an official shot of the three judges for the Guild archives.

On her way home, she dropped the film off at The Banner for overnight developing so she could submit something to Brad and start filling the photo album record of the special quilt show. When she tapped on the glass window of The Banner office, Luther jumped up from his desk and loped over to the front door, letting her in. He had hoped she would drop by. He'd been watching Grama's Quilt Shop and the apartment above to see when the lights came on indicating someone was home. They were both smiling broadly and Susan gave him a quick and chaste peck on the cheek as she stepped past him.

"Do you have time to develop these photos tonight, Lu?" she asked holding out the rolls of film.

"You bet," he said cheerfully. "For you. Anything, anytime. Would you like to stay and help?"

Under the friendly scrutiny of his amorous attention, Susan's face blushed warm pink all the way to her soft blonde hair. At first, their mutual interest in photography had brought them together in casual conversation—one as a professional, the other as a talented amateur. Then they had started dating a couple of months ago. Susan had to endure her sister's inevitable teasing about what went on in the darkroom when the red 'Do not enter' warning light was on. But Luther was a gentle and attentive, even shy, boyfriend, and she enjoyed his humorous companionship. As Clareville's only newspaper photographer, Luther was well-connected and well–known around town. Susan was comfortable and at ease with his circle of friends.

It was a pleasant way to end the day, working through the evening on a project with the lanky young photographer.

Four

For the first time in its history, the Clareville Quilt Show, 'Pieces of the Past', is a juried show. As part of their Fifteenth Biannual celebration the Guild commissioned three nationally certified adjudicators to evaluate the quilts. There was prize money to be awarded, donated by nationally known quilt suppliers and local businesses, and the Guild did not want any accusations of bias or favoritism to mar the show.

Audry Mills was the first judge to arrive in town, having driven in the night before and stayed at a friend's home. She's been judging shows for three years, whenever she can get away from her four– and six–year old. She is a well–known teacher and quilter in the region and is a soft–spoken woman with short curly brown hair. "Quick to laugh and slow to boil", is how her husband of twelve years describes her. Audry's quilts have been featured in several magazine articles and she is just completing her first book of patterns, to be published in May.

Her specialty is 'wearable art', the trendy phrase for quilted clothing that more accurately describes the exotic and creative inventions that quilters and fiber artists are designing these days. Her spectacular and colorful outfits are the complete opposite to her self–effacing demeanor.

In contrast, Beryl Carter was a quilter "before it became so popular", as she says. She is a tiny woman, with steel–grey short cropped hair and wears stylish red–rimmed glasses. Her friends call her "The Roadrunner" because she never sits still and is always on the go, here and there and everywhere. A passionate and demanding teacher, many of her students are now equally well–known teachers. She was one of the first officially certified quilting judges and helped write the adjudicator's manual for quilting standards.

Tom Lansdowne started life as a history teacher, married a quilter and caught the bug. A native of Clareville, now living on the West coast, he and his wife, Sybil, run a mail order quilting business, and although he admits he had never taken a stitch in his life, he is fully committed to the quilt as art, and as a heritage handicraft. He's been consulting with the Smithsonian Institute for several years, wrote a book on the history of Wisconsin quilting (Sybil's home) and has been judging shows for ten years. He's also presenting a series of lectures on the history of quilting as part of the conference at the Clareville show.

Despite the chaotic move–in and general confusion, by six thirty most of the vendors had completed their preparations and had gone home to supper or to their hotel. The judges were assembling in the hall. The quilts were hung and all the many helpful workers had left.

Most people don't realize when they walk into the neat and tidy, orderly and polished, beautifully completed quilt show just how many people it takes to put the show together. There are many hidden hands whose work is largely unnoticed and unappreciated. The greatest amount of work always rests with a small group of guild members. They are inevitably the first to arrive and the last to leave. They bear all the headache–inducing, decision–making responsibility.

They are usually the heads of the committees and sub–committees. There is often little reward for all the hard work, except the satisfaction of sharing their love of quilting, and the pride of seeing the wonderful quilt show set up and ready for the public.

The honor of being in attendance at the judging therefore fell to four women: Carmen, the current Guild President; Rosemary, this year's Quilt Show Chairwoman; Joan, the founding President of the Guild; and Betty, the head of the quilt hanging crew. This gave them the pleasant opportunity to walk the Show in peace and quiet, and to study the quilts and make whispered comments.

Throughout the walk, Betty kept up a quiet but incessant nervous chatter. Her jocularity was a little too forced. The other three knew that Betty had a stunning quilt of her own in the Show and that it was a contender for one of the top prizes. Her agitated state was understandable and they felt kindly toward Betty's jumpiness.

The last task the women had to perform before the judges arrived, was to pin a blank piece of paper over the name of the quilt and the quilter, obscuring its identity. This was done so that the judges would not be influenced by the work of any particular quilter, either positively, or negatively. Like in a court of law, evidence of prior offenses is not permissable. Not always possible, particularly for well–known quilters with an inimitable style, or for a quilt that has been 'on tour' to a number of shows, or that has been featured in a magazine article.

Every attempt is made to ensure the anonymity of the quilt-maker. The quilts are identified by numbers only. The judge must not be able to say, "I know this quilter can do, (or has done), better than this". There are no claims of 'temporary insanity' on the part of the quilter if a quilt goes wrong.

The judges must evaluate each quilt on its individual merits. This is fair. It provides an 'even playing field' for everyone. Quilting standards, like any standards of excellence, need to the be same for everyone.

Unfortunately, this is also unfair. It pits amateur neophyte quilter against semi–professional fiber artist. And let's face it, most quilters are amateurs. Not that what they produce is amateur–ish. Far from it. But most are not trained artists *per se*, trained in the use of color, or how to draw, or in perspective. Most quilters learn as they go, often re–inventing the wheel at each step, hopefully gaining belated techniques and ability with each quilt. So, a quilt that might be considered an excellent effort if produced by a new quilter, in such an anonymous blind–folded judging, could be marked down as an inferior attempt if made by an experienced quilter.

Is the answer to expand the categories to differentiate amateur from professional quilter? Do you add categories that segregate entries by experience of the quilter? If you do, are you not then judging the quilter, rather than the quilt itself?

The point of entering a quilt contest, or any quilt show, is not to win. It is to participate. Like in a kindergarten race, where everyone who crosses the finish line receives a winning balloon, everyone is a winner. Some are just a little faster, that's all. Every stitch is a winner. Some are just a little smaller, that's all.

Every fragile creative ego needs to win. Women understand this so well. It most probably was a mother who invented the balloon–for–everyone race. Perhaps because we have all been mothers who poignantly watched our little ones valiantly dash for the finish line, only to see the earnest little hearts broken when they didn't 'win'. Or perhaps we were once the little ones ourselves.

Every quilter wins when they participate. The grow through the participation and what they learn from it. They get to take pride in the creative work they do, to have it admired by their quilting peers and envied by those who don't.

Whenever possible, at juried shows, the judges provide individual written critiques of the quilts. This is an onerous task, both in time–consuming effort, and in the struggle to be fair, helpful and encouraging. A criticism of poor workmanship to a beginner could depress them and put them off quilting forever, or at least deter them from ever entering another contest, and thereby preventing them from ongoing improvement that comes with the joy of quilting. The same criticism to an experienced quilter could needfully spur them to improve the quality of their craft and propel them on to more difficult challenges. The blind judging, not knowing the level of the quilter, calls on the utmost diplomatic skills of the judges. Sometimes their attempts to be tactful end up in obscurity for the recipient.

In order to complete all the written evaluations, the three judges divided the task. Most of the quilts were hung in alcoves formed by the pipe–and–drape dividers, one quilt to each of the three sides. Each judge took one quilt from every alcove of three and wrote a critique of the numbered quilt on an evaluation form. These would be given to the committee who would pass them back in a sealed envelope to the appropriate quilt–maker. The comments are confidential to the quilter.

The three judges who came to Clareville had been asked to decide on winners in several categories, determined by the Guild committee. There was prize money commensurate with each classification. Each category requires different techniques and presents its own challenges. Hand–quilted, full size quilts. Hand–quilted, wall quilts. Machine–quilted, full size quilts. Machine–quilted, wall quilts. Best pieced quilt. Best appliqued quilt. And overall Best of Show.

Each judge also chose their own 'Judge's Choice' award. This award allows everyone to understand what the individual judge's criteria and preferences, or prejudices, may be.

It took the judges over three hours to complete their assessment. They made a preliminary quick trip once around the show that would eliminate over seventy percent of the quilts, while they simultaneously filled out the individual critiques. Their second tour was slower, stopping only at each of the finalist quilts and marking their evaluation forms. The four committee members followed at a discreet pace behind the trio in order to be helpful if needed.

At the end of the second tour, the judges retired to compare notes and make their decision in private.

"Well, as far as I'm concerned there are only three quilts worth mentioning," declared Beryl Carter, as she slipped her pen onto her clipboard.

"Even if that were the case," Tom Lansdowne replied, "we still have to have a winner in every category. Besides, Beryl, you are always too hard on the entries."

"Standards are standards," she peevishly answered. "This is an old argument with us, Tom. You'd give a ribbon to everyone if you could."

"Not true! Not true. You know that! I just think there are some reasonably good quilts here. This isn't a national level competition. It's a well–known local Guild that has done very well to draw such good entries from across the region."

"Well, nothing here excites me," Beryl shrugged.

"So, we're not talking about standards after all. You want to be impressed. Is that what a quilting competition is all about? Are we on Broadway, or off–Broadway?" he tweaked Beryl, as he stood stroking his beard and his eyes twinkling with amusement beneath his thick eyebrows.

"You've been in California too long," Beryl kidded back. "You've taken that laid–back attitude too far."

"And you've spent too much time in New York. This is the hinterland. This is country, where quilting has its roots. You've become too jaded."

"I agree," Audry finally spoke up. She had been nodding along with Tom each time he spoke. "This is a good looking show. Well set up. Interesting. They have some top teachers giving classes—including yourself, of course, Tom! I would like to have seen more prize money. It might have attracted better quilts, but I know how hard it is to get sponsors to donate. I think they've done well."

"I agree, too," Beryl admitted, still thinking about Tom's last remark. "Maybe I *am* too jaded. Maybe I've been doing this too long. I used to love going to quilt shows. Now it seems like a job. It used to hurt me to make these decisions about other people's quilts. Now, I'm not sure."

Tom put his hand on Beryl's shoulder sympathetically.

"Being a judge is no way to win a popularity contest," he soothed her compassionately. "Sometimes you have to be tough. Let's face it, nobody ever won Olympic Gold because a judge said, 'Gee, she tried hard!'"

"Maybe I should move to California and start a new life, too," Beryl continued. "Or here to the country. Aren't you from around here, Tom?"

"Mm-mmm," he shrugged a noncommital answer.

"It's very pretty here. Last night I stayed with a friend of mine who just moved to the area. What's the town like?" Audry asked.

"Oh, I don't know. I haven't been here in years." Tom shrugged off the questions and started to flip impatiently through the evaluation papers on his clipboard. "In any case. Do you want to start with the Best of Show and work down, or from the wall quilts and work up to Best of Show? We're going to run out of time if we don't start making some decisions."

"I like process of elimination best. Let's work up to Best of Show," Audry suggested. "I like to remember the last quilt I see as the Best of Show."

Tom nodded.

"Sounds fine," Beryl agreed and they set out to decide on the winners.

As Beryl indicated, the judges were looking for specific standards of technique in the quilts. They were looking for accuracy in stitching, and piecing, seams straight and even and overall lay–flat completion. In the quilting, it had to be small, evenly spaced stitches whether it was hand– or machine–quilted. They would also want to see experienced use of color and fabric. A quilt is something that is 'of a piece', where each element must coordinate and cooperate with all the other elements. Colors should be chosen not only to define the block patterns of the design and the desired visual effect, but also to help express the mood and tone of the quilt. The number and design of the fabrics used should also reflect the intention behind the quilt, and not overwhelm it.

Beyond technical merit, the judges were also looking for a certain quality of creativity and vigor. They want to see innovation, or, if using a traditional pattern, to see it handled in a new and interesting manner. They wanted to see the character of the (anonymous) quilter expressed in the quilt. Finally, it had to incorporate, or be indicative of, the show theme in some way.

In the end, there were three quilts vying for the Best of Show ribbon. The judges decided to have one last look at the three finalists.

Cathy Wanamaker had submitted a meticulously pieced quilt of combined *Ohio Star* and *Storm at Sea* patterns. She had cleverly super–imposed the two traditional designs and created an optical effect. Her quilt was a 'scrap' quilt with dozens of individual fabrics in a blue–white–black color scheme. One of the most popular quilt colors, blue and white quilts are hard to resist for their fresh, sparkly appearance. Cathy's piecing was precise and accurate and her quilt was expertly and heavily hand–quilted. It was certainly a show–stopper. Her quilt was appropriate to the 'Pieces of the Past' theme of the Show because it was a 'pieced' quilt, and, because the designs she used were traditional, historical patterns, used in a modern way. It deserved to be a finalist.

The long-awaited quilt that Gladys Brock submitted turned out to be a hand–appliqued quilt of her own design. Unique designs are always a point–gainer. It depicted a gay pastoral scene of two young women and a young man riding in an old convertible car along a country road. The scene itself, being set back in time, qualified the quilt for the Show theme. She, too, had expertly used dozens of different fabrics in the details of the trees, clothing and car. Because of the busyness of the design, her hand quilting was less extensive, but complemented the theme nevertheless. It was a work that could be the highlight of her quilting career, or of any quilter's career.

As the judges stood in front of this second quilt, Audry noticed that Tom was frowning deeply and rubbing his beard. He hadn't started to mark his evaluation sheet and was staring intently at the quilt.

"What's the matter, Tom?" she asked in concern.

"This quilt," he replied slowly. "There's something about it that seems familiar to me. Sort of a *deja vu* feeling. I wonder if I've seen it before," he mused and then breathed heavily. "Oh well, it doesn't matter. It's an excellent quilt."

It will probably turn out to be one of Marion Masters' quilts, he thought and tried to shrug off his uneasy feeling with a rationalization. She was a California quilter he knew whose work was always popping up unexpectedly in shows around the country.

"I just hope it isn't a copycat quilt," he sighed. "We'd look pretty foolish awarding it top prize if it's a copy of someone else's work."

The third finalist, Betty Harrison's quilt, was also an applique. Another of her trademark Baltimore Album quilts. She had made three already and was well experienced in all the detailed technique of hand applique. Because of the complexity of the designs, 'Baltimores' also tend to be show–stoppers. They are quilts that tend to smack you in the face and say, "Yes, I *am* spectacular!" Even non–quilters can appreciate the amount of intensive labor that goes into creating one. Looking at one Baltimore can be exhilarating, but seeing a whole show of them, or even a dozen displayed at a time, becomes mind–numbing. After a couple, you just can't take in any more of the exhaustive, and yet static, intricacy. They become, in the words of the British, 'a much of a much–ness'.

Although technically competent, Betty never creates her own patterns, preferring to use the tried and true, and well–known, Baltimore Album motifs. But what the quilt lacked in originality was made up in expertise and traditional heavy quilting. Baltimores are also historical quilts and therefore naturally fitted the 'Pieces of the Past' Show theme.

Like signatures, every quilt is unique and different. It's a difficult decision for quilt judges. Like comparing apples and oranges, they are both excellent fruits but personal preferences can't help but be part of the decision–making. In the end, even with universally agreed–upon guidelines, decisions can be arbitrary and even whimsical. Rarely does a panel of judges agree unanimously. The verdict is always a compromise.

The judges job was completed by ten o'clock and it was near eleven by the time the committee was ready to leave. After the judges had announced their decisions and left, the committee had to remove the pieces of paper obscuring the quilters' names and to pin winning ribbons on the appropriate quilts. Betty was all fumble fingered as she handed pins to the other women. It was an embarrassing situation.

Joan thought it best to tackle the issue straight on.

"Sorry you didn't win Best of Show," she said kindly to Betty, who was putting on a brave act in the face of her defeat for the sake of the rest of the committee. Betty had won Best Applique quilt, but not the coveted Best of Show. Rosemary put her arm around Betty's shoulder and hugged her friend warmly.

"It's OK," Betty replied with forced brightness. "Gladys' quilt is really spectacular. She deserved to win. It's a *wonderful* quilt," she said as she busied herself nervously with the adjudication paperwork. "I can't wait to congratulate her. I knew as soon as I saw her quilt that it would win," she smiled faintly.

Betty offered to decode the designated quilt numbering system and place each of the written judges' evaluations into sealed envelopes for the various quilt–makers as the other committee members moved the Best of Show quilt to a featured position and another quilt was moved into its former spot. Everyone sensed that would be the kindest thing—not to have Betty's nose 'rubbed in it' by having to move someone else's quilt into the winning circle.

"Good decision," Carmen commented once they were out of earshot, as she and Rosemary and Joan took down Gladys' quilt with its Best of Show ribbon. "I think this is Gladys' best quilt ever."

"Funny she decided to do an applique this time. She always does those intricate pieced quilts," Joan observed.

"I'm glad," said Rosemary quietly. "At least Gladys is prepared to try something new. I think Betty is in a rut with her Baltimores. They are all beautiful. But I'm tired of them. I really hate it when judges automatically give the prize to a Baltimore. It's as if it were the only kind of quilt worth emulating."

"You know, that's a thought," Joan said reflectively. "I've always said to myself, 'Someday I'm going to make a Baltimore. It will take me twenty years to do it, and then I'll die!' I have always considered them to be sort of the epitome of quilting. I'm sixty–three now. If I don't start one soon, I'll never get it finished!" She laughed at herself.

"If we all live long enough to complete all the quilting projects we have in mind to do, we could live forever," Carmen smiled ruefully.

"She's putting on a brave face but I'll bet Betty is some ticked off that Gladys won Best of Show. I know they try to be civil, but they've never really liked each other," Rosemary commented. "Personally, I think Betty has always been jealous of Gladys' quilts. I can't recall any show in the last few years where Betty won in any category that Gladys had a quilt. And come to think of it, hasn't Gladys won the Viewer's Choice ribbon the last three shows?"

"I think you're right," affirmed Joan.

"At least she's trying to be a gracious loser," Carmen smiled as they carried the quilt to its new honored location and rehung it. Her voice implied, "and that's all we should say about it", so their conversation turned to other matters.

Finally, satisfied that everything was ready for tomorrow, the senior committee members gathered their bags and prepared to leave for home.

"How are you getting home, Joan?" Carmen asked as they made their way to the hall door.

"Going with Rosemary," she replied pulling on her overcoat.

"I can take you," Betty offered. "You're not that far from me, You're all the way across town, Rosemary. I can take Joan."

"Are you sure?" Rosemary asked. "Thanks. I wouldn't mind getting a little more sleep tonight. If you don't mind."

"No trouble at all," Betty reassured them. "Just let me go to the bathroom before we leave. When my bladder hits that cold car seat, we'll have an accident. I'll just be a sec." She walked briskly back to the washroom.

"She's being awfully nice about all this, isn't she?" Rosemary repeated as they slowly walked to the front doors, allowing Betty time to catch up.

In a couple of minutes Betty joined them and all four women left together, waving to the security guard as they left. "We're the last," they called out to him. John waved back, picked up his keys and headed for the quilt show hall. He had just come on duty and had been waiting for the all–clear signal, having already double–checked the back access doors.

Inside the front door of the exhibit hall he reached over and turned off the banks of overhead fluorescent lights, leaving the more dim incandescent potlights still on. The room was shadowy and still. In all the booths around the perimeter, merchants had old sheets and long swatches of fabric draped over their wares to dissuade any idle fingers from temptation. John smiled. No one had ever had anything stolen after hours from any of his shows.

It was a small feeling of pride that he could hold onto. He liked this job, a night job. He didn't have to deal with very many people, and even those he did, he could keep at a safe distance. John had come home from Vietnam with a whole body but he had left something of his heart behind. Once he had been a dynamic, even aggressive young man who pushed himself to the limits whenever possible. The horror of war had rapidly stripped away the shell he walked around in and John was now a much quieter, thoughtful man. He found it hard to relate to people who hadn't gone through what he had. He just wanted to live a quiet and uncomplicated life. Every day he was just glad to be alive.

As he walked slowly around the hall, the soles of John's heavy brogues creaked rhythmically on the carpet. He didn't hear them, though. Clipped to his leather belt was a pocket–size walkman, and on his head he wore the thin wire headphones. He listened to the ballgame as he ambled slowly around the hall making a last security check and admiring the quilts. It was an Angels' game from the coast. His favorite team was in second place only one game behind the hated Oakland A's, but if they didn't pick up, their chances of the pennant were growing slimmer. Absorbed in the quilts and the third, bases loaded inning, he also didn't hear or see a pair of white sneakers move around the back corner of the hall.

The Angels left the runners stranded as the batter fanned. "Ach, damn," John muttered under his breath. He slid the headphones down around his neck irritably, turned on his heel abruptly and moved to leave the hall in disgust. As he reached the front door, he reached over and flipped off the remaining light switches.

"Oh! Wait!" cried a voice from inside the room. "Wait! Don't you dare lock me in!" joked a woman coming forward into the beam of light that was streaming into the darkened hall from the foyer.

"You're here late! I thought everyone had left," John apologized and held the door open for her. "I didn't see you. Sorry!" he said as he glanced down at the stranger. She was wearing a green vendor nametag so she had authority to be in the hall.

"I was just putting the last touches to my booth," she panted, explaining as she slid by him out the door. She had been pulling on her overcoat as she approached him and now she was struggling with fastening the buttons with her gloved hands. "There wasn't enough time to have everything ready before the Show opens. Will you be here in the morning? What time can we get back into the hall?" she asked with a frown.

"Show opens at nine. Vendors can come in at eight. That's when I leave," John replied over his shoulder as he locked the banquet hall doors and rattled them to make sure they were secure.

"Oh dear," the woman fretted. "Any possibility I could get in just a *few* minutes earlier than that? I have so much more to do."

"Sorry, m'am," he shook his head. They started to walk

toward the front entrance doors. "But you know, it probably won't be too busy, first day an' all. You should be able to finish up even after the show starts." John smiled at her kindly. Must be her first show, he thought, they're always so nervous first time out.

"Well, OK." She forced a grim smile. "I'll be here right at eight. Good night."

"Night, m'am. Safe home," he waved and watched her walk to her van in the breath–freezing night air. John then locked the front doors, put his headphones back on and returned to his office.

The fortress was locked securely for the night. The drawbridge was up. Inside the treasure waited patiently for the adventure–seekers to arrive in the morning.

Five

The Quilt Show opened on Thursday morning. It was a clear cool mid–October morning. 'Frost was on the pumpkins', as they say. Unlike any other time of year, Autumn in the country lives up to it's patchwork metaphor. The trees blaze warmly with a storm of yellow, rust and red color, interrupted by cooler patches of deep pine green and pale, dying, brown–green. It's a liminal time, a between–time on a threshold from what's been to what will become. Summer's exuberance is giving way to Winter's hibernation. It's a time of death, with the confident assurance of Spring's rebirth to follow. All things must pass away, for growth and creation and life to cycle onward.

The early morning newspapers hit front porch steps and paperboys left warm black footprints in the white rime. Businessmen left cars warming in driveways, spewing clouds of billowy steam in the predawn light. Bedroom windows ran with wayward rivulets of frost–condensed water as children dressed for school.

On all the major routes and intersections around town there were signs and posters declaring 'Quilt Show Today' with directions to the Community Center. That's good, Angela thought, as she noticed the signs on the drive to the Quilt Show. LeaAnn's publicity committee had been busy late last night, planting the encouraging signs.

At seven o'clock, John stretched and arched his back while

seated in the old swivel chair. The novel he had been reading lay upside down tented on a wooden desk that was pushed against the wall between a filing cabinet and a bank of metal lockers. His second coffee had grown cold, so he dumped it into the small sink in the corner of his closet–sized 'office'. He felt sluggish and sleepy. Every hour during the night he had made his rounds of the community center complex. He marched slowly from his office to the hall, pool, rink and back to the hall and his office, rattling doors and checking window frames as he went. With boring regularity, nothing ever happened. Unless you count the time some hooligans tipped over the trash cans out back. More noise than calamity in the end, but it had made his heart thump wildly anyway. Just the possibility that anyone could be breaking into his territory made him react to the sudden staccato as if it were gunfire.

Although the heat in the community center is controlled by a computer, John automatically made his way to the maintenance room and checked the dials from habit. Then he unlocked all the inside access doors and the wooden doors to the banquet hall in order to save time when everyone arrived. There's always someone waiting impatiently to get in, he thought, and remembered the woman from the night before. He unlocked one loading dock door in the back, poked his head out momentarily, half expecting to see her, and then made his way to the front entrance doors. He didn't like to appear out front too early when he knew it was likely people would already be there. It seemed mean not to let people in when it is cold outside. But rules are rules. And after all it was his job to be strict and assure the security of the place.

Sure enough, three of the Guild ladies and a vendor were waiting. At two minutes to eight, John opened the doors and secured them in the unlocked position.

"Mornin' ladies," he smiled. "Everyone ready for a busy day at your show? Looks like fine weather for the weekend."

"We hope so," said Angela, carrying in boxes of doughnuts and muffins. As Merchant Mall Chairwoman she was providing morning and afternoon refreshments for the vendors. "Join us for a coffee and doughnut before you leave your shift, John?"

"Thanks, but no. I have a full tank of caffeine already," he chuckled. "I'll be lucky if I can get to sleep this morning."

"Lucky you. Wish I was going home to bed," LeaAnn smiled. "We were up until after three last night."

"I thought you had everything in hand. Did it take that long to put out the signs?" Carmen frowned.

"Oh, it wasn't work. 'Lavinia'–Sue is staying at my place. After we put up the signs, Leslie, Joan, Freda and Beth came over for a gab session. She is so funny. We were in stitches. No one realized what time it was!" LeaAnn explained.

Just then Beth and Joan caught up to them, followed by Annemarie.

"We were just telling Annemarie what a great time she missed last night," Beth recounted to the other members.

"How come you didn't come over?" LeaAnn asked. "It's not like you to miss a party."

"Well, something came up," Annemarie said tersely. "Besides, I couldn't have stayed up that late anyway. I need my sleep." She waved them brusquely away, walked over to the registration table and began setting up her paperwork.

"Did someone rattle her cage?" Beth joked quietly to LeaAnn. "She may have slept but it didn't help her disposition this morning." LeaAnn just shrugged and headed for the kitchen to help put on coffee and set out refreshments in the merchants' hospitality room.

In the next half hour, the hall would quickly fill with busy people. Vendors opened their booths, taking down the covering sheets, firing up their cash registers, and making last minute adjustments to displays, in an anticipatory flurry. There was a great deal of friendly, pre-show excited chatter.

The out-of-towners:

"Where did you eat last night?"

"We found a great Chinese food place."

"Want to go out one night after the show?"

"Love to. If it's a good show." (Meaning, if I can afford to.)

"Are you going to be at Charlestowne next week?"

"It was full. I couldn't get in."

The locals:

"There's a Halloween sale at The Barn this week."

"Meyer's has chicken on for twenty nine cents a pound."

"Did you hear Dr. Gorman has sold his practice? I hear he's moving to Florida."

"I didn't know he specialized in geriatrics!"

Committee members fanned out to their various stations and duties. The first crew of white gloved volunteers ambled idly around the silent quilts.

By eight thirty, everyone had arrived and the Show was ready to open to the public. There was a hushed and happy excitement in the hall.

Outside, there was already an eager lineup at the door waiting to get in and get started! The Registration Table was located to one side of the front door outside the banquet hall where the quilt exhibition was. Treasurer Carol Anne Rafferty was manning it along with her two assistants. Any one who entered the hall would have to be wearing either a one–day stamp on their hand, or a blue nametag with their name and their class code numbers printed on it, or a green nametag for vendors. As a special commemoration, anyone attending classes was given a canvas carrybag emblazoned with the Clareville Quilt Guild name and the 'Pieces of the Past' logo for this year's show. Everyone else had to buy them.

Just inside the hall, near the door, was the Raffle Quilt Table, run by two other Guild members. The revolving wire mesh drum was already one–third full from advance ticket sales. Beside them, two other Guild members sold special Show pins that quilters love to collect and proudly wear, like hard won war medals, representing all the quilting skirmishes they had survived. Many quilters even make special 'collars' or scarves that can be worn over any outfit, eliminating the need to pin and repin dozens of show pins. The real serious quilters make, or buy, a 'chatelaine', to carry not only their trophy pins but also their quilting tools—scissors, needles, spools of thread, and all–important thimble.

Morning of the opening day at the show is a busy one. Quilters come to register for their classes, to pay any outstanding fees and to have their first quick look at the show and to shop for any supplies they may need for their hands–on classes.

There's a mysterious art or science to attending a quilt show. Everyone has their own favorite pattern, depending on how much time they have been able to carve out of their lives to devote to the selfish pursuit of quilting. Whether they have one hour, four hours, one day or four days, they have to see it all, and so they will pace themselves according to whim and personality.

There are those who will arrive first and early to shop. They want to make sure that they find the best treasures at the show before whatever is coveted is all sold out. A good likelihood, since there are so many hundreds of bolts of fabric available and yet vendors can only bring so much with them. If you miss getting your yardage of that special new fabric, you may just lose out on it forever. Sometimes the early birds even forget to look at the quilts, or do it as an afterthought at the end of the day. They come prepared, with large empty bags.

Others will come to see the quilts first. They want to have their visual senses and imaginations kicked into gear before they make any purchases. Unless they received or brought heavy canvas carrybags, they will delay their buying until just before leaving so they don't have to lug anything but ideas around all day. They come prepared, with notepads and cameras.

Some quilters need to see everything first before they make their final decisions—afraid they will run out of their allotted money before they see that absolutely must–have item later in the show. They may have to make several trips around before narrowing their wish list down to their can–do budget.

Others will move systematically around the show alternating from quilts to vendors and back, keeping an even balance. They will only go around once and be gone, until next year, next show.

Many quilters travel in packs. Like wonderful howling wolves. "Ah-ooo," they beckon each other. "Ah-ooo. Come SEE this!"

"This is a-MAZ-ing!"

They goad each other on. "I already bought something. You buy something now!"

"One yard is never enough! You better take two just in case. You'll never match that color again. Ah-ooo!"

Others are lonely stalkers. Like sleek cats on silent paws, they ooze in and out of booths, carefully observing every detail, uncommitted until they pounce. Perhaps reaching out a tentative finger to pat a shiny bauble. They stand frozen in front of a particularly diverting quilt, studying their prey like lions in the long grass. They tense up their creative muscles in concentration, and then, suddenly, they pounce and grab their quarry, the elusive bird of inspiration.

Some are earnest and totally absorbed in the serious business of looking at quilts, thinking about quilts, sneaking a touch whenever possible. Still others visit the show as a picturesque backdrop to a delightfully social day out with friends, gabbing about everything *but* quilts.

A few drafted spouses cavalierly escort their obsessed ladies around the show. They busy themselves taking the official photo memories and lugging carrybags. They are always at least four booths or six quilts ahead of their short–legged, long–focussed partners. Advance scouts, perhaps, but usually looking for interesting items to lure their wayward partners forward, forward, forward.

Some are called 'the fabric police' affectionately behind their backs. They never understand why she needs *any more fabric*. They never understand why it takes her *so long* to look at one quilt.

A quilt show is where quilters can wear their quilted creations—jackets, vests, skirts or country style homespun dresses. All embellished, or embroidered, or otherwise uniquely crafted clothing. Nowhere is there a more appreciative audience. If you wear your gorgeous one–of–a–kind outfit to any other social gathering, it could be dismissed as just something you bought at Lord and Taylor. Wear it to a quilt show, and everyone knows that you made it yourself. People will stop you in the aisles to comment on its loveliness, to examine an intricate detail, or to ask wherever did you find that material.

Whatever outfit she is wearing, the quilter will be wearing comfortable shoes. There is an expression here: 'Fashion stops at the knees'. Everyone knows it will be a long day on their feet and they dress accordingly. At any other friendly gathering, if you take a group photo for a souvenir and you cut off the feet of everyone in the picture, your photographic skills are forever afterward mocked as cockeyed. At a quilt show, you are *supposed* to cut off everyone's feet in the photo! That is the proper etiquette. Those comfortable old sneakers just don't go with that gorgeous quilted skirt and jacket.

Eventually everyone comes to a quilt show. Quilters, wanna–be quilters, used–to–be quilters, and just plain quilt lovers. Even families come, with babes in bundles or toddlers in strollers. Which makes the "white glove" ladies and the vendors nervous. Everyone is on the alert as any potentially sticky or chocolate covered little fingers approach. A whispered signal will telegraph its way along the line preceding the small invaders. "Watch out for the women in the purple jacket. Her kid's eating a chocolate chip cookie."

Most shows are posted with No Food, No Drinks signs, but inevitably there are lapses, mostly from strangers unconscious of the damage they could cause to the quilts or wares in the show. One hand touching a displayed quilt isn't much. Multiply one hand by several hundred show–goers and you have a soiled and grimy quilt at the end of the show. The white glove ladies are the quilt police, whose duty it is to remind everyone to look, not touch, and by wearing her white gloves allows anyone to view the back of any quilt by handling it carefully herself.

In any event, by the end of the day, everyone will be glassy–eyed. Too much to see and think about. Feet are sore. But if you don't leave a quilt show foot–sore and brain–dead it just hasn't been a good experience. Everyone *expects* to go home hungry, exhausted, and inspired.

The Fifteenth Biannual Clareville Quilt Show hall was

comfortably full of early attendees by nine–fifteen. True to their word several bus tours from neighboring guilds were lined up at the door slowly being ticketed into the hall. Thursday, and Friday, would be popular days with retired women or at–home Moms, who could get away during the weekday and avoid the weekend crowds.

The Banner photographer, Luther, was getting ready to take pictures. Susan was acting as his unofficial assistant and trainee. Mayor Brown had arrived at the front of the hall in order to officially open the Show and to make his tour of the quilts. 'Uncle Al' Brown had a great knack for getting his face in the newspaper. Which was one of the reasons he had been mayor for so long. One week it would be on the society page at a charity tea, the next on the sports page with the local high school gridiron champions. His office in the town hall was directly opposite, across the old town square park, from The Banner streetfront office. One assumes the Mayor spent many a morning coffee break staring down from the second floor window at his free publicity agent across the way, and planning how he would meet this week's print deadline with a photographic or quotable event.

It was just then that Minnie Winterspoon, one of the white–gloved volunteer ladies, scurried up to Carmen Sanchez, who was busy talking with one of the vendors, and tapped her on the arm.

"I have to speak to you," she said breaking into the conversation.

Pulling Carmen aside, she said behind her white glove into Carmen's ear, "Where's Gladys' quilt?"

"It won Best of Show," Carmen replied. "We moved it to the

back to the special exhibit area."

"No, no! I know it won! They told me that this morning! But it's not there now!" Minnie asserted.

"What do you mean, 'it's not there'?" said Carmen. "Of course, it's there! I helped rehang it last night before we all left!"

"Well, I'm telling you, it's not there now," said Minnie. "Come see for yourself!"

The two women went off toward the back of the hall. Carmen ws waylayed several times by happy quilters expressing early congratulations on the magnificent quilt show the Guild had produced. After all the hard work, it was a wonderful boost to finally hear such accolades. It was difficult for Carmen, with Minnie in tow, to break away and keep moving toward the back display area. When they finally worked their way to their destination, Carmen stopped suddenly in her tracks.

Minnie was right. There was the special eight–foot pipe–and–drape section with a cordoned area around it where the Best of Show quilt should have been hanging.

The drape was empty.

"See!" gestured Minnie, triumphantly.

Carmen stood puzzled for several seconds. "Well, what could have happened to it?" she asked herself and the thin air. "I'll find out," she told Minnie abruptly. "Just go on to your station."

Carmen headed to the front doors quickly and this time with purpose. She collared several committee members. Everyone was as unbelieving and puzzled as she had been and the group made its way again to the empty display. No one seemed to know what to say, as they stood there numbly staring at the void.

"Has anyone seen Gladys this morning?" someone finally asked.

No one had.

"Do you think she removed it from the show?" Another person trying to sort out the puzzle.

"Why would she do that?" another challenged the suggestion.

"Not likely, either. Since no one has seen her yet this morning, I'm not sure that she even knows she won. I called her late last night but got no answer. Besides, she knows that if she takes the quilt out of the show, she won't receive her prize money," Carmen commented.

"This is bizarre," one voice muttered.

"We better look around the Show first. Who knows what could have happened?" LeaAnn suggested, having joined the ever–growing group of worried women.

"What's up?" asked Marion Cooper, one of the vendors who wandered by and was intrigued by the gathering.

"There's been a quilt stolen!" someone answered.

"We don't *know* that it was stolen," Carmen asserted. "Let's not fly off the handle! Carol Ann, please call Gladys and see if she has anything to say about it. Everyone else look around."

"What did it look like?" Marion asked.

"Good question," someone commented. "I never saw it. Gladys didn't deliver it to the committee until late yesterday. She was being so darned secretive about it."

"It was an applique quilt. It had a scene on it of people riding in a car," Rosemary said, rubbing her forehead, recalling the quilt.

"Should we look in the vendors' booths?" someone asked.

Several vendors had quilts to sell, including antique ones, and it would have been fairly easy to secrete the quilt among the many folded and piled quilts in a booth. The assumption that it had been stolen was already forming in people's minds.

"Yes. I suppose we have to," Angela replied. "But be *tactful* about it. Let's not go accusing anyone. Let's just assume it was *misplaced accidentally*."

"The important thing is to find it," Carmen agreed.

"What do we do with the display in the meantime?" Joan asked.

"I'll make a little sign," Rosemary offered, and the group dispersed to hunt for the missing quilt.

The search eventually took on ridiculous proportions. Having looked in all the obvious places, they began looking in the least likely places. All the storage rooms were checked, even though no one had been into the rooms. All the empty quilt shipping bags were checked, even though everyone knew they had been emptied the day before when the quilts were hung. Committee members walked the show several times, hoping to see the quilt hanging somewhere where it didn't belong, even though Carmen and Rosemary had both been present when the prize–winning quilt had been rehung in its place of honor.

An hour later, nothing had turned up. By then all the vendors had heard the news, and, that no one had been able to contact Gladys Brock, the woman who had made the quilt. It was a mystery.

In the end Mayor Brown had his picture taken in front of the missing display, posed with his hand extended, palm open, into the empty space. Much to the annoyance of the photographer, it had taken the mayor several minutes of inner debate whether to be shot smiling or not. With the threat of no photo at all, he quickly decided on a suitably sombre expression. This week it would be on the front page.

"Why would anyone steal a quilt?" Horace Roundtree, of "The Temple of Templates", asked Angela, whose booth was beside his. In addition to organizing the Merchant Mall, she had her own booth to staff as well. Jennifer was unfortunately away for the weekend. But Susan, who had kissed Luther goodbye for the day, was now helpfully doing booth–sitting duty, lending assistance to their temporarily overburdened Mom and her fulltime shop assistant.

"Makes no sense," she replied. "What can you do with it? Can't sell it. Everyone's going to know what it looks like."

"Well, not necessarily," he replied, thoughtfully. "It wasn't ever featured in a magazine and someone said this is the first show it was entered into. Gladys might not have even taken a picture of it herself."

"This seemed to be a special quilt for her, too," Angela added.

"True. But you know someone could easily remove the label from the back," Penny Prescott of "Penny Cotton", offered helpfully from her booth on the other side of Angela's. "It could be sold in New York..."

"Or California, I suppose," Angela interrupted.

"...and passed off as someone else's work," Penny finished.

"What a shame. To go to all that work and have it stolen like that. Gladys is going to feel terrible," Horace shook his head sympathetically for the absent quilter.

"Does the show have insurance?" someone asked, joining the discussion.

"They have to," informed Horace knowingly, "but it only covers liability for personal injury. It doesn't cover theft. It's up to the individual quilter to have their own work insured. Most don't bother. It's never usually a problem."

"Well, I have all my quilts insured," said Marion who had wandered over from her booth, "The Antique Attic".

"But you would have to," Angela pointed out. "because it's your inventory. You sell antique quilts. It's a business cost. Horace is right. Most quilters don't even list their quilts on their household insurance policy, much less have them insured separately."

"Unless it's a valuable antique quilt or a family heirloom," Penny suggested. "And yet even then..."

"Right. It's hard enough to get quilters to even sign and date their quilts. Getting them to have them evaluated and insured is next to impossible," Horace said. He shrugged as he started to walk away. "So, I guess it's her own fault. Nothing we can do about it anyway."

And so it went for the morning. Guild members and vendors all exchanging insights, opinions and gossip. At first the committee tried to keep the news quiet and not tell the public. The sign that Rosemary had installed in the empty display space read: "This quilt has been temporarily removed from exhibit." It was the 'temporarily' that drew everyone's attention. It sparked the inevitable questions.

"Why was it removed?"

"When will it be returned?"

Many of the townsfolk who visited the show were well acquainted with committee members, and the local vendors, so ultimately talk spread. It was impossible to keep the news quiet. And once the newspaper carried the story it would be known by everyone anyway. Eventually, all who entered the hall knew that the Best of Show quilt had disappeared mysteriously.

It was certainly a stirring way to start a quilt show.

At eleven o'clock, Rosemary Campbell decided that it was her duty as Quilt Show Chairwoman to call the police, but it would be another two hours before anyone showed up. In the meantime, morning classes finished and the all–day classes broke for lunch. There was another wave of telegraphed rumors and a throng of quilters came over lunchtime to stand and look at the empty display and conjecture.

Shortly after one o'clock, Judy Marshall, the Deputy Sheriff, finally pulled up in her squad car. Judy was a thirty–something career police officer. She had the clipped and officious sounding voice and mannerisms that policewomen acquire at the academy, that say 'Take me seriously, *I'm* armed and dangerous'. The fact that in Clareville, police officers didn't carry guns, failed to change her demeanor. Otherwise cheerful and gregarious with her friends, Judy would become guarded and distant in any official capacity. The dark tinted aviator sunglasses she wore helped her to hide any unseemly emotions.

Thursday would have been Judy's day off, but unfortunately Sheriff Jeff Bob Burnet was away on vacation, and she was left in charge of the station, and the rookie officer, Jeremy Brown. It was bad enough that she was bogged down with all the extra paperwork, but this was Jeremy's first posting, and Judy resented baby–sitting him. He had graduated last in his class. Well, somebody had to. Clareville took pity on him and gave him a job anyway. His uncle, *Mayor* Brown, was duly grateful to Sheriff Burnet for the familial favor.

Jeremy was earnest enough, just a yard short of a bolt, that's all. He had taken the call from Rosemary, and dismissed it as relatively unimportant. He hadn't wanted to interrupt Judy's battle with the mountain of paper, and set it aside. It was the 'relatively' that made Judy mad when she found out, and that got him chewed out as she quickly left the station.

Judy's concession to working on any day off, was to wear blue jeans, a black turtle neck sweater and a pair of scuffed tan cowboy boots. It didn't matter what she wore, everyone knew this was an official visit.

As Judy entered the Quilt Show hall, Carmen stepped forward to greet her as the official Show organizer. Judy was momentarily surprised to see her.

"Hi, Carm. Long time no see. What's happened here?" Judy asked taking a notepad from the pocket of her black leather jacket. She passed over the familiar pleasantries abruptly. She felt uneasy talking with Carmen now. Judy had dated Carmen's brother Luis a few times, at Carmen's instigation. He was charming and good–looking, albeit short, but he turned out to be an implacable chauvinist. The kind of guy who would be out cattin' around on you on your wedding night, she had decided. Judy dumped him, and now it was awkward meeting Carmen. But Carmen bore no ill-feelings toward Judy.

Carmen tried to explain. "We feel really silly calling you on this, Judy, but one of our prize–winning quilts has vanished. I'm not sure what we should do. And we haven't been able to locate Gladys Brock."

"Is that the woman who made the quilt?" Judy asked.

Carmen nodded.

"Any possibility she just decided to take it away herself?" Judy asked, hoping for the obvious and easy answer. "Is there anything stopping her from doing so?"

"No, she could if she wanted. It's just that no one saw her here at the Show after she dropped the quilt off yesterday. All the quilts are left in our charge and we are very careful. There is a great deal of confusion and coming and going during the set–up but I saw the quilt last night myself. And the hall was locked up last night, of course. This is so upsetting," Carmen said, fretting and wringing her hands in angst. "Nothing like this has happened at one of our shows before. I don't know how we'll tell Gladys. This was a special quilt she made for this show."

"Don't worry," Judy assured her. "I'm sure it's all easily explained. There's no use panicking. It's not likely that someone actually stole the quilt. We'll find out what happened. You better give me all the details first."

Twenty minutes later, having taken down all her notes for a report, Judy drove over to Gladys' house to talk to her. There was no reply. Assuming that Gladys was out shopping or running errands, Judy was unconcerned, and made a note to drop by in the evening.

She wasn't sure what she could do about the apparent theft. Even though the hall was locked up last night, the quilt exhibition was a public show with access by countless people this morning. Sometimes all it takes is brazen audacity. The public would be unpleasantly surprised to know how often valuable objects are lifted, right under the nose of people who just weren't paying attention, or weren't suspecting. Moving vans full of thieves have walked off with whole houseloads of furniture without neighbors even lifting an eyebrow, much less the telephone.

In the meantime, Judy called John, the security guard, and woke him up. After introducing herself officially, she explained the reason for her call.

"I've been at the quilt show at the community center and apparently one of their quilts has come up missing. I wonder if you can shed any light on it."

"It can't be!" he exclaimed. "Everything was locked up tighter'n a drum! Judy, give me fifteen minutes, and I'll meet you there."

"Now, John," Judy calmed him down. "Don't *you* start to panic!"

"I'm not. But I know that if the quilt was there when the committee ladies left last night, then it didn't disappear when I was on duty. It has to still be there. I won't be able to sleep now anyway.

I might as well be there," he said with finality.

John dressed quickly and with rising agitation. He folded himself into his rusty '64 Triumph Spitfire and gunned the motor as he backed out of his crowded garage. On the way to the show, John thought about everything that happened last night. He tried to recall whether he could possibly have missed any lock or window, or whether there had been any noise that he didn't investigate. He came up blank.

Then suddenly he remembered the woman that had been at the Show late last night.

"I almost locked her in the hall," John told Deputy Marshall when he arrived. "Other than the committee, she was the only person in the room."

"You say she had on a vendor nametag? Would you recognize her again?" Judy asked.

"Probably." John thought about it. "Yes, I would," he decided, recalling details of her height and weight. He remembered that she wore glasses, and a cap, and, the gloves. It had to be her, he thought to himself. No one puts gloves on before they put on their coat. It was a little straw to grab onto. It hadn't been important at the time but now it seemed obvious.

Together Judy and John walked the show. John wanted to see if he could recognize the vendor. They were joined by Charlie, the day security guard, and Carmen Sanchez.

As they approached "The Quilt Peddlar" booth, they witnessed a quiet but heated conversation taking place between the vendor and a customer. When the customer saw the four of them, one in uniform, apparently bearing down on her, she turned abruptly and left. Judy's eyebrows went up in surprise.

She introduced herself and asked the booth owner, Dixie, "What happened?"

Dixie laughed but she was clearly annoyed.

"She was copying one of my designs," she explained. Dixie designs her own quilt patterns. She sells them along with kits and wooden quilt holders that her husband makes. Her designs, like all original designs, are automatically copyrighted and it is theft to reproduce them without her permission.

"When I saw her standing there with a notepad copying down my pattern, I politely asked her to stop and pointed out that she was stealing my idea. But she ignored me. Twice I asked. I guess when she saw the security guard's uniform she thought she was going to be in trouble and left."

"Does that happen often?" Judy asked, wondering if there was a connection or a tendency toward pilfering work in effect here.

"Not really, I guess. Most people are terribly honest. And after all, a pattern only costs a few dollars, so quilters buy them. Every designer knows that they will probably share the pattern with friends and that's the cost of doing business. Like one person buys a book and gives it to four friends to read. It's just some people are so blatantly rude that they would have the nerve to copy an original design with the artist standing right there."

"It's an old problem," Carmen pointed out to Judy and then turned to Dixie. "Doesn't every creative act follow on and take inspiration from previous creative acts?"

"Yes, of course. To a certain extent. We all influence each other's work. But a detail–for–detail copy is theft." Dixie shrugged her shoulders in resignation and said finally, "My consolation is that in all likelihood the woman will never actually do anything with the idea."

Dixie was obviously not the person he was looking for so John was anxious to move on, and had started toward the next booth. The others were drawn along with him. Judy made notes and then followed a few steps behind.

In the end, they stopped at every booth and spoke to each vendor in order to give John an opportunity to recognize the mystery woman he had seen and briefly spoken to the night before. He didn't find her. He was starting to doubt his recall. Sometimes his focus and his memory just wasn't as sharp as it used to be. After a while, all these quilting ladies started to look alike. There were too many people in the hall and he began to feel hot and claustrophobic. A feeling he hadn't had since the nights in the overwhelming jungle. A panic started to rise up inside him and he excused himself from the group to catch some fresh air.

He sat on the steps outside the back loading dock doors for several minutes, breathing deeply and holding his forehead against the cold metal framework of the handrail. He didn't notice anyone outside with him until a man's voice said gently, "Are you alright?" And he looked up to see a tall man smoking a pipe standing over him.

"Yeah," John breathed.

"It gets pretty close in there," the man said, knocking the ashes out of the pipe against the opposite railing. There is a No

Smoking rule at all quilt shows, so he had obviously stepped outside for a smoke. The man was watching John carefully but unobtrusively as he slowly and carefully scraped out the pipe.

"Yeah," John breathed again. "Gets to me sometimes."

"All that noise bothers me, too. All the voices in there," the man motioned over his shoulder toward the building. "Ever see *Apocalypse Now*? Reminds me of that sometimes."

"'Nam," John said simply, and the older man nodded his head sagely.

"Yeah. I see," he said compassionately.

John looked him in the eye. He did understand. It made John feel better.

"I'm OK now. Better get back inside. There's a quilt been stolen. We've been investigating it," John explained, as he stood up.

"Oh? I hadn't heard. I've been in class all morning and then back at the hotel. What happened?" the man asked as he pocketed the pipe and reached out to open the back door. The two men introduced themselves and John explained as they went back inside and joined Judy and the others.

"Judy. This is Tom Lansdowne. He was one of the judges last night. We were just talking about the missing quilt. Tom, this is Deputy Sheriff Judy Marshall."

"Yes. Hello, officer. I was saying to John that when I viewed the quilt last night I thought there was something disturbing about it. I couldn't put my finger on it. Maybe it isn't important but it seemed familiar somehow," Tom shrugged, trying to explain his uneasy feeling, then waited for a response.

"Could it have been a copy of something?" Judy asked, remembering the conversation she had with Dixie.

"Well, I thought so at first. But somehow I don't think so. I just don't know," he shrugged again. "I guess that isn't much help."

Judy made a note. "Thanks. Everything helps. Sometimes we just don't know how."

Tom nodded and excused himself from the group.

While John was outside, Judy had been introduced to the Merchant Mall Chairwoman, Angela Patten, and she asked her if there were any other people who would have had vendor nametags.

"Only their helpers," Angela explained. "Every vendor is given extra nametags for friends or relatives who are going to help them set up. You can't get in without a nametag."

"During the set–up," Charlie explained. "There was no other event going on at the center on Wednesday, so only the loading dock doors were open. The front doors were locked so there was no other way in but through the loading dock and I was there all day. No one went in or out without proper I.D."

"What time did you leave, Charlie?" Judy asked.

"Around five–fifteen," he replied. "The two part–time evening guards come on at five. The center is always busy in the evenings, so there are two men on then," he explained. "They are both good men and I'd vouch that they did the same checking of anyone entering the hall."

"I'm sure. I'll talk to them anyway, Charlie. Write down their names and phone numbers for me," she directed, then turned back to Angela. "I'll need to talk to the vendors' helpers. Do you know who they are?"

"Yes. We have a list of all the names that nametags were requested for. I'll get it."

It was later than she realized. Judy had been working on this 'relatively unimportant' call for several hours. She was still at the community center when Charlie went off duty at five o'clock, so Judy was able to question the evening security guards. After that, John, Judy and Angela made another tour of the show. By then it was near six o'clock and the show was preparing to close for the day.

They asked each vendor if the extra helper nametags had been used, when the person was present during set–up and what time they had left. Did anyone see someone wearing a nametag that didn't belong? It was a fruitless question, since many of the vendors didn't know each other that well, and they wouldn't necessarily recognize a stranger as being an intruder.

Finally, some light was shed when they spoke to Roberta Walker, of "Scratchin' to Patch". Roberta had rented a triple–sized booth and had six helpers. But when she checked in at the vendor registration table there were only five nametags in her envelope. She had to have an extra one made on the spot.

"That's right," Angela declared. "I forgot about that. I don't know how we missed making out the sixth tag, but I assumed we had made a mistake and since Roberta was right there with her six people, we went ahead and made up another tag."

"That means someone could have taken out a nametag from Roberta's envelope sometime beforehand," John remarked.

"And that means, anyone could have had access to the hall,"

Judy observed. "All they had to do was wait until the committee left. It could be anyone," she declared. "There's no way to know who it was."

"But how did she get the quilt out of the hall?" John asked defensively. "That woman wasn't carrying anything. She said she was coming back early this morning to finish up her booth."

"A red herring perhaps," Angela suggested.

"It might mean that the quilt was still here in the building. Hidden. She could have come back anytime today and carried it out in a carrybag. John, you were off duty, so she didn't have to worry about being seen by you." Judy shrugged. "End of mystery. Unfortunately."

Judy shook her head. "There doesn't seem to be much to do about it now. We could search the whole building again and every package that leaves but frankly I just don't have the time or manpower to do that. I suspect that it is long gone now anyway. Sorry." Judy flipped her notepad shut with a message of finality that she was leaving. Having spent the entire afternoon on this wild goose chase, she was tired and annoyed. She would still have to file a full report on the incident.

"Well, thanks anyway," Carmen sighed.

"I'm still trying to get a hold of Gladys," Rosemary commented. "I'm not looking forward to telling her how this happened."

"I'll stop in to see her on my way home this evening," Judy offered in consolation, feeling a little guilty for her impatience. "Sounds like you did everything you could to insure the safety of the quilts. You just can't protect yourselves against everything. I'll try to reassure her."

"You don't know Gladys!" Angela laughed and shook her head. "Good luck!"

The group dispersed and the Show closed. Everyone went to home or hotel conjecturing about the missing quilt.

John had several hours to occupy before he would be on duty at eleven. He drove downtown to Ivy's restaurant and sat thinking over last night and today's events. He felt bad about the theft, right under his nose so to speak. Before Charlie left the center this afternoon, he had tried to console his colleague.

"It's not your fault," Charlie assured John. "The woman had a proper nametag on. What could you do? Who'd suspect these little old ladies to be up to such larceny?" Charlie tried to joke his friend out of his bad mood.

It was obviously going to lay heavy on John's mind for a long time. He wouldn't be listening to the ballgame tonight as he walked his rounds. A question would continue to nag at him all through the worrisome, restless night: how and when did the woman take the nametag from the envelope? It had to have been before the show set–up. Who had access? Couldn't it only have been one of Angela's committee members?

He didn't like the answer to that question and it bothered him that he would have to ask it tomorrow morning.

Six

Judy headed home for supper, planning to eat before heading back to the office again for more paperwork. She liked Sheriff Burnet but she had discovered after he left for vacation, that he had also left a pile of *his* work unfinished, that she had to slog through. There's more papering than policing in this job, she thought irritably. But still, she reasoned with herself, it's a far cry better than her last posting in the city. She'd grown up on a farm outside Clareville, thought she was escaping to the 'big smoke' as a young ambitious woman, and now found it pleasantly comforting to be back in Clareville.

When she got over her brief snit, Judy put together a salad and opened a can of flaked tuna fish to toss into it. Inspired, she opened the fridge and took out a bottle of black olives, chopped some up, and sprinkled them over the bowl of greens. "There you go—Nicoise," she said to the large, hopeful dog watching her. "You don't like fish," she pointed out as he followed her, as she took the bowl and a fork and a can of root beer into the livingroom and sat with her feet up on the coffee table while she ate.

Questions plagued Judy all through her supper. Did the mysterious woman just take the best quilt in the show, or did she take that one particular quilt? If the former, she would have had to wait until the judging was complete to know who the winner was, before removing the quilt. If the latter, how did she know the quilt was going to be there? And, of course, why that particular quilt?

They were questions only Gladys Brock would be able to answer, so at eight o'clock Judy loaded Rufus, the dog, into the car and drove over to Gladys' house. Rufus wasn't hers. He belonged to her brother, Mike. He, too, was a policeman, a Detective in Montgomery. The dog had helped him solve a case and so he decided to keep the stray. But Mike was in Europe on his honeymoon, so Judy was dog–sitting for a month.

From the road, Gladys' house was dark. Still not home, Judy thought. She hummed the opening bars of the song 'Stand By Me', 'When the night has come, and the land is dark, and the moon is the only light you see...', while she thought.

"What do you think, boy?" Judy asked the attentive mutt seated next to her. "Would she be gone all day like that, and, all evening too? On the day and night of the quilt show opening? If you entered a quilt in an important show like this, wouldn't you want to see whether or not it won?" she asked him.

"Yeah, I think so, too," Judy nodded her head in response to Rufus' single, throaty, "Woof". She got out of thc car and approached the small, one storey frame house. The house was set back twenty feet from the sidewalk and there was a low decorative fence surrounding the well–kept lawn. As she walked up the front steps Judy could see that all the curtains were drawn.

Judy rang the front doorbell, lightly tapping her fingertips on her right thigh as she waited. There was no sound of movement from within. No answer. No lights on anywhere. She stood back.

"Ah, I hate it when this happens," she said to the dog that was busy sniffing the porch floorboards, as if checking to see who had been visiting here lately. The hairs on the back of her neck were itchy and her stomach was sinking. Judy's intuition alarm bells were ringing loudly but she tried to ignore it.

This time she knocked on the door, vigorously, and insistently. Nothing.

Finally, she walked back down the steps and across to the neighbors' houses. She asked the neighbors on either side and directly across the street if they had seen Gladys today, or this evening. Judy wasn't surprised that no one had seen her.

"Not good," Judy said to Rufus as they walked between the houses, debating what to do next. Her questions had aroused the curiosity of the neighbors who were now watching her subtlely from behind curtains, or overtly from their front porches.

"Do you think she's alright, Officer?" called out a man from across the street.

"Well, we're beginning to wonder!" Judy yelled in reply.

She went to the door and knocked one more time. She put her hand on the doorknob and it turned. To her surprise it opened.

"Stay," she commanded the dog, pointing her finger at him. Rufus sat down but stood up again as soon as Judy turned away and started to move into the doorway. She sighed at his disobedience and finally just pushed him out the door with her knee on his chest as he tried to lean in after her. She closed the door and called out to Gladys.

No answer.

"I didn't really expect anything," Judy said out loud. I wish Jeff Bob was here, she thought. Her heart was beating fast in adrenalin–pumping anticipation. So far it had felt good to be left in charge during the Sheriff's vacation, despite the paperwork and Jeremy. But this was one time she wished she had someone else to call in and assist her. Judy had a bad feeling about what she was going to find.

Shining her flashlight on the wall near the door she located a switch and turned it on. She walked a few feet down the hall and turned left into the livingroom, again turning on a light as she entered.

"Oh dear," Judy sighed as she saw a woman's body on the floor. This was undoubtedly Gladys. For some reason Judy had assumed that the quilting woman was an elderly lady and expected to find that she had a heart attack.

Gladys was sprawled face down on the floor, on an old Axminster carpet. A coffee table and teacups had been scattered and broken in the process. A pool of dark blood had oozed out from under the body.

Judy moved toward the body and gently rolled it over.

"Oh, oh," she said. A large pair of sewing shears with black handles was sticking out of Gladys' blood–soaked chest. "Oh God," Judy groaned. "Well, now it's a different story," she said.

"Well, at least I don't have to tell her that her quilt was stolen." Judy tried to use humor to distance herself from the upset she felt at finding the body. It's a sight no one ever gets used to. She sighed again as she touched her neck and confirmed that the woman was dead, apparently for quite some time.

Moving to a side table Judy pulled a plastic glove from her

pocket and put it on before picking up the telephone and calling an ambulance. Then she went to the front door. She put Rufus in the car.

Ignoring the curious neighbors, she returned to the livingroom and walked around the room. From another angle, as she looked back at Gladys' face for the first time, she saw that she was probably much younger than she had thought, around forty or so, wearing extremely heavy makeup. A false eyelash had rubbed off on the carpet. Blood had dried on her cheek where it had dribbled out of her mouth.

Judy's head started to race with questions and procedures. She pushed the questions aside for the time being. Don't touch anything, she told herself. She pulled out her notepad, flipped it open and started taking down detailed notes about everything in the room. Maybe the coffee table was knocked over in a struggle. A lot of 'maybe's' started to emerge. This complicates things, she thought, and then realized she had to call in the homicide police force in the city. Clareville just wasn't equipped to handle this sort of situation.

It took the ambulance half an hour to arrive at the house. There was no emergency since the woman was already dead, so a heart attack call across town took priority. It gave Judy a chance to start her own investigation. She checked the house out for a possible break–in. There was no evidence to suggest forced entry.

"Oh, Gladys, Gladys, Gladys," Judy shook her head. "You must have let the perpetrator in yourself. Did you know him or was it a door–to–door salesman you let in? Was it even a 'him'? What about a 'her'?" Judy asked the silent corpse, remembering the mysterious quilt–stealing woman from the show. Is there a connection here, or just coincidence, she wondered.

When the ambulance pulled up at the curb, she had to have them wait for the homicide squad to arrive before they could remove the body. Annoyed, the drivers checked Gladys to confirm that she was indeed dead, and then sat impatiently in the van. She knew homicide would officially take over the case. In the meantime, Judy returned to her car and retrieved her camera. She wanted to take her own photos of the crime scene.

She went across to the persistently curious neighbors and told them Gladys was dead, but not how. It didn't seem to abate their curiosity at all, but she wasn't prepared to discuss it with them. One of the powerful auras of police officers is that they do the questioning, not the answering.

The city squad finally arrived, took pictures and fingerprinted everything in the room, the door knobs and door frames, and then prepared to go away again. It was perfunctory and quick.

"Robbery probable motive," one of the city squad declared closing his notepad.

"But there was no break–in!" Judy argued.

"Little old ladies will open their doors to almost anyone," the uniform shrugged.

"She wasn't old, and it doesn't look like anything was ransacked or taken!" Judy prepared to battle.

"Got scared off by something before he found anything worth taking," he shrugged again.

Judy shook her head in annoyance. "You're going to write this whole thing off, aren't you?" she accused.

"Did you know this woman?" he asked.

She shook her head. "No!"

"Do you have any reason to suspect anything but robbery?" he asked, finally suspicious of something, of Judy.

Judy opened her mouth to speak, to tell him about the quilt theft, but suddenly decided she didn't like this guy enough to share her information with him. "No," again, softer.

"Fine," he said. "Can you handle the next of kin, and so on?"

"Yes," Judy replied tersely.

The disinterested homicide squad left. The impersonal ambulance drivers removed Gladys to the county hospital morgue pending an autopsy and final arrangements by the family.

Judy sat down carefully in a wingback chair in the suddenly quiet and empty livingroom. She felt distinctly uncomfortable now that everyone had left, including her would–be hostess.

"Next of kin," she told herself and directed her attention to locating Gladys' handbag where hopefully she would find an address book. It's reassuring to people like the police that we all live such predictable lives. A man carries his life in a wallet on his hip or in his briefcase. A woman carries her life in her handbag. We're easily investigated.

Judy found the purse in plain sight in the bedroom, removed the address book and Gladys' keys and replaced the purse securely in a dresser drawer. As an afterthought, she pulled it out again and checked the wallet. There was fifty-six dollars and change still in it.

"Yeah, right," she smirked. "Robbery, my butt."

She put the purse away again, flipped her notepad shut and slipped it back into her jacket pocket. She was finished here for the night, and made her way to the front of the house turning off lights as she went. Softly she shut the door behind her and locked it with Gladys' key.

Climbing back into her car Rufus came over to lick her face. "Blechh!" she said, pushing away his eager snout. "Dog germs!" she complained aloud.

As they drove away, it was apparent to Judy that it was going to be even more important to find out who took Gladys' prize-winning quilt. And why.

Judy wasn't the only one thinking about Gladys' missing quilt. On the other side of town, Tom Lansdowne was driving to an address scrawled on the back of a sales slip. He was going to have a drink with an old high school friend. Ever since he had seen Gladys' quilt during the judging, he had been bothered by something. At the time, he didn't know she had made it, of course, but once he found that out, and now that the quilt had disappeared, he was more curious and concerned than ever. It occurred to him to call Gladys, but he really didn't know her personally. Candice was the only person he knew, to talk to about it.

Most of Clareville's downtown streets were still familiar to him, but the newer suburban part of town was a maze of twists and cul–de–sacs that confused him in the darkness. He had arranged to meet Candice at eight-thirty but it was closer to ninewhen he finally pulled up at her gate. He walked briskly up the long driveway. Her bright smiling face popped into the window of the front door when he rang the bell.

"Oh, *Tom*! It's you," Candice exclaimed, as if she were surprised to see him. "Come in, come in. It's so good to *see* you." She smiled sweetly as she gestured him to pass her. She closed the door behind him and a waft of her heady Shalimar perfume reached him.

Tom noticed that she looked different than she had the other day at the show. Her long red hair was loose and curly around her shoulders. Tonight she was wearing tight blue jeans and a pink lambswool sweater with a low cut V–neck. She still had a figure that could stop traffic, he noticed, and tried not to. He began to feel uncomfortable when he realized he was alone in the house with a very attractive woman. As she led the way into the livingroom, her high heel mules made a flip–flapping sound with each step. There was a gas fire hissing in the fireplace—it was the kind of immaculate room that you wouldn't want to truck real logs and ashes through. The room was dimly lit with indirect lighting and Mantovani music was playing seductively in the background.

"Sit down," she invited, and gestured to the couch, and he did so, straightening his tie as he sat. Candice stepped out of her mules and instead of sitting on the chair opposite him, she chose to sit beside him on the sofa, turned sideways with her knee bent and one bare foot tucked under her. She laid her right arm along the back of the couch with her hand resting just beside his shoulder.

"It's good to see you again, after all these years," he said in genuine friendliness. "When I saw you the other day, it got me thinking about the old days at Central High."

Tom had been the star quarterback for the Panthers. She was

head cheerleader and in their senior year had been elected Homecoming Queen. A gorgeous young woman then, still stunning now in middle age.

"Yes, I think about those days at lot, too," she smiled. "They were 'the best of times'," she quoted and gestured expansively. A charm bracelet jingled attractively on her slender arm.

"And the worst of times, too, remember," he smiled, but a cloud had passed over his eyes. There were serious things he wanted to talk to her about.

Sensing his mood had changed, she jumped in quickly to keep the evening upbeat. "I'll never forget that game against Northern Tech. You were brilliant! Everyone said it was the best game they'd ever seen. You looked so powerful in your uniform. And you are still such a handsome man, Tom." Candice touched his shoulder lightly with her fingertips as she spoke.

Her touch evoked a memory in him. He remembered that she had a crush on him in high school. The resurfaced memory made him uncomfortable. One year she had stuffed supposedly anonymous love notes into his locker. But everyone knew she had set her sights on him. It was embarrassing. She had been pretty and vivacious, but he was attracted to someone else, and the more she tried to attract his attention, the more he ignored her. He hadn't thought about those high school days for a very long time. Tom was uneasy with her flattery and he moved to change the subject.

"And you've done well," he remarked as he gestured around the well–furnished room. "Your own interior design business. I'm not surprised. 'Candy Cane's Country'. I like the name. Someone told me you got married," he said, looking around the room, hoping for evidence of another man.

"Yeah," she shrugged. "No one you would have known. After you left Clareville, I had to settle for second best." Her laughter was brittle and forced. She continued to be uncomfortably familiar with him. Tom disliked the sarcastic turn of the conversation, that implied an intimacy that hadn't existed. "It didn't last," she continued blithely. "But that was then, and this is now. There's no point hashing over that old stuff."

"I agree. We all have to move on," he said pointedly, leaning away from her as he spoke. Twisting himself slightly sideways, he mirrored her position, with his left arm on the back of the sofa, elbow bent and his head resting against the back of his knuckles of his closed fist. Placing his left ankle on his right knee caused his left knee to stick out toward Candice. It was an unconscious barricade to prevent any further physical contact with her. It also allowed him to look at her straight on without turning his neck all the time. Anyone reading his body language would interpret it as saying, 'I'm open and friendly, but don't touch me'.

"I got married, too. Sybil. She's a Wisconsin girl. A wonderful wife. We have three children. Jason has gone to Princeton this Fall."

Tom continued to talk about his wife and children, hoping that talking about his contented home life would make it clear to Candice that he was a happily married man.

She got the message and thought to herself, then why are you here, honey? In her mind, this was their opportunity to make up for all the lost time.

"That is just wonderful, Tom," Candice interrupted him. "I'm so *happy* for you," she effused. She had been making an attempt to listen attentively and then gushed enthusiastically when he stopped to breathe, but she was tapping her long red fingernails on her knee as he spoke. The irritable fingers belied the smile on her face. She didn't want to hear about some other woman and her brats.

"We have a mail order business," Tom carried on. "Funny that we would both end up in a quilting related business, eh? Speaking of which..."

"Oh, we probably still have a *lot* in common, Tom," Candice interrupted with an encouraging smile. "I'll bet your favorite drink is still Remy Martin, isn't it. In fact, why don't I fix us one?"

She stood up without waiting for his answer and headed toward the kitchen. By then Tom was decidedly uncomfortable with the situation and didn't know what to do about it. He realized that somehow he had to get out of there, but how to do it without hurting Candice's feelings? He was feeling hot and wanted to wash his face.

"May I use your washroom?" he called out to her as she pushed through the swinging door into her kitchen.

"Of course! Down the hall, second right." She smiled with satisfaction as she mistakenly interpreted his action as a prelude to intimacy.

Tom rose and walked down the dark hall rubbing his forehead. He was getting a headache. He had wanted to talk to her about Gladys' missing quilt but it was clear she had other thoughts for the evening. He opened what he thought was the bathroom door and walked in, closing it behind him. He was inside before he realized that he'd made a mistake and was in a bedroom. He was turning to leave again when something shiny caught his eye. It was a photograph in a frame on a low dresser. The gilt frame had reflected the light from two votive candles burning on either side of the picture. His curiosity heightened, he moved closer to see who Candice was honoring in this way. When he stepped up to the dresser he was horrified to see it was a picture of himself, and her. He picked up the heavy gilt frame. It was an enlargement of their Homecoming Ball. As the star quarterback and Homecoming Queen they had been photographed together for the yearbook.

Tom was stunned. He reeled a step backward as if he had been punched.

On the dresser he could see the Central High 'Clan Call', his yearbook, *their* yearbook, opened to where the photograph was. The page was marked with a silk ribbon, and a dried corsage had been pressed between the pages. It was the traditional honorary corsage he had presented to her, the Homecoming Queen.

This is unbelievable, he thought in a panic. She couldn't have been carrying a torch for me all these years, he denied the thought.

"This is too bizarre," he whispered out loud. Tom felt his stomach heave as his head began to spin with memories and questions. His head was splitting now and he had to leave. As he stepped backward, he twisted, tripping on the loose throw rug and half fell to the floor, catching himself with outstretched arms. Standing up, slightly bruised and sore, he stumbled backward into the hall, spun around and forced himself to walk straight to the front door. He paused momentarily with his hand on the doorknob, wondering if he should speak to her. Politeness was such an inlaid habit with him that despite his revulsion he was actually uncomfortable leaving without saying goodbye. He could faintly hear Candice in the kitchen chopping vigorously at an ice cube tray and singing cheerfully as she dropped the cubes into an ice bucket.

"Don't be a damned fool!" he admonished himself and opened the door.

Candice had just emerged from the kitchen bearing a tray with a bottle of cognac, two snifters and icebucket. She was looking down, carefully balancing the tray.

"Here we go!" she said brightly. "Hope I didn't keep you waiting too long!" She looked up just in time to see the front door shut quietly.

"Tom?" she said, puzzled.

There was no reply. She moved forward and placed the tray on the coffee table.

"Tom!" she called out down the hall toward the bathroom. She went to the front door, looked out the panc of glass and saw the tail-lights of his white rental car pull away from the curb.

"Oh, Tom," she whispered plaintively. She turned around and leaned her back against the door. Tears started to stream down her face. She stood there sobbing quietly into her right hand. With her left hand, she reached over to the wall, fumbled for the switch, and flicked the porch light off.

Tom pulled away from the curb as fast as he could. He was

sick and appalled that Candice had constructed what looked like some sort of shrine in his honor, apparently in her bedroom. He kept seeing the candles burning, like an eerie eternal flame, illuminating the photograph, as if it were something more than a staged formal high school ritual. She must be crazy, he thought, to keep that stuff displayed like that.

This is too bizarre, he kept repeating to himself.

He hadn't been able to talk to her about the quilt. That was important. He had to ask her about it. There was something that bothered him. And Candice's behavior had bothered him. His head was swimming with the thoughts of the quilt on one hand, and the thoughts of Candice's obvious seduction on the other. Thoughts, and ideas, and questions, were tumbling around inside him.

The way Candice had acted reminded him of something else he had forgotten. And suddenly he realized what the theft of the quilt meant. It was so obvious. Just like a cartoon light bulb going on over his head.

"Oh, no!" he exclaimed as he slapped his hand on the steering wheel. He kept shaking his head, no, no, no, denying the thought that had finally fallen into place for him. No wonder the quilt had bothered him so much at the judging.

Tom had been driving on autopilot for several minutes. When he came to his senses and focused out the window, he realized he had gone the wrong way across town to the hotel.

He was lost. So when he saw the welcome sign of the gas station, he stopped for gas and asked directions. He had to backtrack until he found the right, familiar road, and then proceeded back to the hotel.

Minutes later, he pulled into the parking lot and walked immediately to the lobby door, checked at the front desk for any messages from home, and went up to his room. He didn't notice the red sports car that had been sitting in the back shadows of the lot, waiting for him to return.

Tom entered his room, loosened his tie, took off his jacket and threw it onto a chair in the corner, kicked off his shoes and started pacing the room in torment. What should he do about what he now knew, he agonized. Should he call the police? But he couldn't prove anything. Who would believe him?

"I need a drink," he said aloud and went to the telephone.

He dialled room service. "Send me up a bottle of Remy Martin, please. And one snifter. Yes, ice, please. Thank you."

He hung up the phone and paced again, running his hands distractedly through his hair. He could see Gladys' quilt clearly in his mind's eye. And he knew that he was probably the only person in town who knew why it had been stolen. Why it *had* to be stolen.

Tom was still pacing the room debating what to do when a knock came at the door and the muffled voice called out, "Room service!"

At last, he thought, and went to the door.

Seven

The second day of the Clareville 'Pieces of the Past' Quilt Show dawned bright and sunny, just as the weatherman had predicted. There was the usual early morning Friday drizzle of local business traffic, nothing out of the ordinary. All over town people headed for work blithely ignorant of the death of Gladys Brock. Children headed for school down quiet streets, unaware of the deathful stillness wrapped around her small house.

Other than the long–gone homicide squad and the unconcerned ambulance drivers, there was only one person in Clareville, other than the murderer, who knew a death by foul play had occurred.

Judy woke up early with a headache as a load of questions started to pound into her brain. She laid in bed listening to the annoying alarm ring and finally pushed herself to sit up, swinging her feet over the side of the bed, before slamming her hand down on the offending clock. Rolling out of bed, she stumbled into the shower to wake herself up and get ready for work. She padded into the kitchen, towelling dry her hair. In the kitchen she let the patient dog out the back door, set the kettle to boil, put out the dog's food, and then let Rufus back in before returning to the bathroom to blow–dry her short dark hair. Finally dressed in her casual work clothes and bolting a tub of low fat yogurt for breakfast, Judy made an instant coffee in a travel mug to go, rounded up her gear, and Rufus, and headed for the office.

She dropped the film off at the lab on the way. The Clareville Sheriff's office wasn't big enough to have a police lab of its own, but they had a good relationship with a local photoshop owner. He handled all their official film. Being an ex–cop himself, he could be counted on to be quick, and to treat their material as strictly confidential.

"You're a good companion," Judy said affably to the wag–tail dog. Walking with Rufus at her side into the police station, she realized that being a policewoman was a lucky job. She could have a pet dog with her at all times and people would think he was an official police dog. Maybe I should get a dog, she thought. They're less maintenance than a husband, easier to house train, and, from her experience, more loyal.

Judy's first call was to the coroner's office, where she left a message on his answering machine. Judy's family had known Doctor Terrell for many years. He was a tall white–haired man with a straightforward and honest manner. There was a kindness in his touch that he gained from the many years he served as country doctor to the rural areas around Clareville. Immeasurably overqualified for the job, he had originally trained as a surgeon in Boston. He was in his fifties when the new community hospital was built and he was offered a position on the staff. His surgical skills had resurfaced in his capacity as county coroner. Judy knew he would be quick, and thorough.

Officially this was a murder, and Gladys' death meant there would have to be an autopsy. She asked Dr. Terrell to call her right away with the results. Judy didn't buy the robbery motive that the homicide squad was prepared to settle for. Label a file 'robbery' and it means ‘case closed’. She wanted to know, as soon as possible, about the pair of scissors, and anything that would point toward a possible suspect. Stabbing someone with their own scissors had to be a pretty spontaneous act, she reasoned. Maybe someone was stupid enough to leave some careless fingerprints.

“You assume they were her own scissors,” her alter ego challenged her. Judy was in the habit of talking over police cases in her head with her fictional counterpart, Sherlock Holmes. Holmes always challenged her assumptions and made her continue to ask questions even after a conclusion had been reached. He kept her from becoming sloppy or lazy in her analysis. “Ah, my dear, but what if...” was one of his oft–repeated provocations.

“If they weren’t Gladys’ own shears, would someone deliberately bring them to do her in?” Judy mused out loud to Rufus, who by then was dozing under her desk. The chair creaked irritably as she leaned back and cupped her hands behind her head. She imagined a silly scene of the cloaked killer dressed like Little Red Riding Hood as if bringing goodies to Grandma, concealing the lethal weapon in her basket, knocking innocently on the front door, calling, ‘Let me in, let me in...’

“‘Not by the hair of my chinny, chin, chin,’ Grandma should have said,” Judy remarked. “Wrong fairy tale, I know.” Judy laughed at herself, and then frowned going deep in thought. “But Grandma–Gladys *did* let someone in... We *do* have a wolf in sheep’s clothing. She didn’t suspect the person. So, who would you least suspect?” There were going to be a lot more questions before the right answers emerged. Even with Sherlock’s help.

After the call to Dr. Terrell, her next telephone calls were all out of town, to the people in the address book. All she could find was the wife of a cousin who was out of town for the weekend. The next of kin business would have to wait until Monday. Poor Gladys, she thought. Dead, cold and all alone for the weekend.

"Reminds me of my own love life!" she quipped to the dog who looked up at her with sad eyes, "As if *you* would know," she said.

After writing out her official report of the quilt theft, and then the murder, Judy went to check on Jeremy. He was duly chastised and was full of spit and polish efficiency this morning. She felt sorry for 'Junior', the name she and Sheriff Burnet had affectionately bestowed on him behind his back. She remembered her own first days on the job in the city. The razzing she got. The mistakes she made. It still made her squirm to recall how clumsy she had been back then. It made things worse that her older brother was already a respected Detective with the force. It appeared that all was in order, and Judy was confident that all was as well as it could be.

Leaving Jeremy at the police station, Judy drove back to the crime scene to interview the neighbors and parked in front of Gladys' house. She needed information on friends or next of kin, and whether anyone had seen anything suspicious the night before or the day of the murder. Judy realized that until she received the coroner's report, she couldn't be sure when Gladys had died and therefore what time of day she was looking for information about. And how did that connect to the quilt theft? Did it take place before, or after, her murder?

Stealing a quilt at least made some sort of illogical sense. But why steal a quilt *and* murder the quilt–maker? Judy pondered the question as she re–examined the scene of the crime. She was looking for anything she might have missed.

After talking with the neighbors, Judy used the key to let herself back in Gladys' small wood–frame house on the quiet side street. It was neat and comfortable. It was obvious that she lived alone. To the left of the hallway was a livingroom–diningroom combined but separated by a large archway. Beyond was the kitchen and back door.

Judy noticed that there were very few family photos. There was one framed portrait of two elderly people, probably parents now deceased. And on a side table was a single framed picture of two smiling girls. One was a dark haired little girl who looked about seven or eight. From the photo on her license, it could have been Gladys as a young girl. The other was a young blonde woman who looked seventeen to twenty years old. The older girl was affectionately hugging the shoulder of the young girl. Too young to be her mother, she decided. Sisters perhaps, Judy wondered. There were no names on the back of the photograph. There never are, Judy shook her head sadly, on photos that are so familiar to the people looking at them every day.

"It's the photos that are always the saddest part," Judy sighed. "You must have left some people behind. Who remembers you?" she asked the little girl in the photo.

Putting the picture carefully back in its place, Judy turned her attention to the rest of the room. The furniture was non–descript and well–kept. On the diningroom table was a partially completed quilt. There were needles and pins and a spool of thread on the table with the fabric.

But no scissors. They would have been in plain sight from the livingroom, she noted.

Several other quilts hung on the walls and neatly folded over chairs in the livingroom. There were quilted placemats on a sideboard in the diningroom. A quilted cosy covered the teapot in the kitchen. Lifting the lid, she could see that it was still partly full of now stone cold tea.

"Is this what a quilter's house looks like?" Judy asked herself. Now sensitized to seeing quilts, she started to notice them everywhere. "Jeez, the whole house is quilted!" she remarked to herself. "I wonder if all quilters are this obsessive?" she mused. The answer would have been yes.

The second bedroom of the bungalow was converted into a sewing room. It was in disarray as Judy entered and started looking around. There were several shelves that contained stacks of neatly folded pieces of material. The walls were covered with old blue floral wallpaper that was mostly covered up with posters, pages cut from quilt magazines with photos of quilts on them, a calendar, and sketches of quilts. For the most part everything looked like it would have been fairly organized, for a workroom. Yet the room looked slightly askew as if someone had rummaged quickly, yet carefully, through everything.

In the center of the room was a large sewing table, with an electric sewing machine at one end and cutting mat at the other. Some sewing tools lay on the table. But no scissors. Judy opened the drawers with her pen, carefully not disturbing any possible fingerprints. The fast–acting bromide of a homicide squad hadn't bothered to dust this room.

"I don't know much about sewing, but I know you have to have some kind of scissors," Judy told herself. She picked up a handle with a round blade at one end and curiously touched her finger to it.

"Ye-o-ow!" she exclaimed, as the rotary cutter sliced immaculately into her flesh. It was so sharp her finger didn't bleed right away, as if it too had been surprised by the incision.

"That's one heck of a blade!" she remarked sucking her finger. "I wouldn't want to meet you in a dark alley!" she said to it, looking at the weapon up close. The steel blade was round so it turned on a pivot point at one end of the handle. The blade was paper thin and deadly sharp, as she had found out. There were some small scraps of fabric on the table, so Judy ran the cutter over one. It severed the material cleanly and easily.

"Hmmm. I'll be darned!" She hummed "Just a jack–knife has old Mack Heath, babe, and he keeps it, out of sight", from *The Threepenny Opera.*

"Is this what quilters use to cut fabric? Maybe they don't use scissors any more."

Investigating further, Judy discovered a button on the handle. Pushing it up ejected a plastic guard that protected the blade end of the cutter, making it safe to handle. Judy dropped it into the pocket of her leather jacket, intending to ask the quilt guild ladies about the device.

So, was it still likely Gladys was killed by her own scissors? If she was, and they were in the diningroom as Judy suspected, it would mean the murderer had to have come into this room, looking for something? But what?

"You were a tidy lady, Gladys," she said out loud. "So how come your sewing room is such a mess? Looks like someone was looking for something," she asked, and answered herself with the obvious conclusion. She waited for Holmes to challenge her but he was silent.

The drawers of a filing cabinet stood open. How am I going to know what is missing, she wondered. What would someone want in a sewing room? They didn't appear to have looked behind or under furniture and the carpet was intact, so the person expected to find what they were looking for out in the open, not hidden under the floorboards.

"What is missing?" Judy fretted the question and sat down in the chair in front of the sewing machine. Looking straight ahead, she noticed there was one large blank in the otherwise covered wall opposite her. A single unoccupied push–pin with a green plastic head was still inserted into the wallpaper. Something had been taken down. Something relevant to the stolen quilt? That wall facing Judy was covered with Gladys' own hand–drawn quilting designs on graph paper. It could have been the plan or design for the missing quilt, the wall suggested to her.

"If you steal the quilt, would you also want to steal the plan for the quilt?" she asked herself out loud. "And why would you do *that*?" she asked again. "Because you don't want anyone to know what it looked like. Why? Why? Why?"

"We're going to have to find out what the quilt looked like, aren't we?" Judy sighed and stood up to leave. She knew it was the end of the quiet investigation time. From now on she would have to disclose that Gladys had been murdered, and talk to people about the crime.

When Judy returned to the office, there was a message from John, the security guard, to telephone him. Before doing so, she put in a call to Sheriff Burnet at his hotel in Atlantic City. He was definitely not a morning sort of person, so she felt sure she would still catch him in his hotelroom before he went back to the blackjack tables. She was right. She woke him up.

Judy explained about the theft and the murder and the homicide squad's case–closed conclusion.

Sheriff Burnet listened thoughtfully, and when Judy finished he drawled, "W'ahl, honey, you know that dog don't hunt. It was robbery all right. But the B&E took place at the quilt show, not her house. I'm sure you're onto something. The two events must be connected. Sugar, do you want me to come back thar and handle things for you?"

"No," she replied carefully. "I'm sure I can handle it, if you agree that we should proceed with an investigation. I'll call you if I have any problems. OK?"

"That's fine, honey." The Sheriff knew he could count on Judy, and he didn't really want to cut his well–earned vacation short, not until he at least broke even, again. He knew she was as good as her word and that if she got in over her head, she would yell for help. The girl had a lot of common sense.

"How's Junior?" he asked. She could hear Jeff Bob smile over the phone.

"Green an' growing," she laughed and rang off. Sheriff Burnet was probably the only man in the world she would let call her 'honey' or 'sugar'. She had learned long ago that he didn't mean any disrespect by it. It was just part of his good old boy speech pattern. In fact, she sort of liked it. He was like a father to her, albeit he was a character, and they got along just fine. His position was an elected one and, strange as that may seem, didn't require any particular law enforcement training. Her position was hired, and J.B. had the great good sense to hire a Deputy that knew something about the law.

The good news was, J.B. had given her the green light to proceed.

When she finally returned John's call, he answered right away. He had obviously been waiting by the phone. He wanted to ask her his question first before going to the Show. "Wouldn't it have to be one of the committee members who had access to the nametags?"

"It's a good question, John," Judy commented. "But things are a little more complicated now," she continued.

Judy explained that she had found Gladys dead last night, murdered, and that she was waiting for the coroner's report to know exactly when she had been killed. John was shocked, to say the least. She told him she was going to go to the Show and talk to the women again, and instructed him not to say anything until she got there.

Poor John, she thought as she hung up the telephone. He felt bad enough about a quilt being stolen. Now I suspect he's going to feel somehow responsible for Gladys' death, too, although, heaven knows, he certainly couldn't have known or done anything about that either. Judy sighed. People are always looking to feel guilty for something. Isn't there enough of the real thing to go around?

It was eleven o'clock. Before leaving, Judy told Jeremy about the murder and that she had spoken to Sheriff Burnet who authorized their investigation, and let him know that because the Quilt Show ended on Sunday she wanted to have the case wrapped up by then, and so he would be on call for the next three days.

"Stay sharp," she said without a smile as a parting comment.

"Right," he replied with a salute that was half in jest but half in nervous subservience.

On the way to the Quilt Show, she debated how to break the news to the Guild members. The less information she told anyone the better, she knew. Arriving at the show several minutes later, Judy located Carmen, who was standing behind the registration table, talking with one of the teachers.

"It's just not like him to be unreliable," Carmen was saying to the woman. Judy took off her aviator glasses and folded them into her breast pocket while she waited for their conversation to end.

"Did you call his hotel room?" the woman asked.

"Several times. No answer. I don't know what to think. We had to cancel his class and refund the students' money. It looks really bad when this sort of thing happens!" Carmen spoke with annoyance and regret in her voice.

The other woman shrugged her shoulders and walked away saying, "Anything I can do to help, let me know."

"What's up?" Judy asked, curious.

"Just another headache. One of our teachers didn't turn up for class this morning. We can't seem to locate him. I would have thought if he had some sort of emergency at home and had to leave, that he would have at least had the courtesy to call someone and tell us."

Carmen sighed with fatigue and put her hand on Judy's forearm. Leaning against her she declared, "I'll be so *glad* when this weekend is over! It's just one thing after another."

"I can imagine how you feel," Judy said sympathetically. She liked Carmen. Despite her brothers, Carmen was an independent, hard–working and caring woman. Which made Judy's task today even more difficult.

"You don't think he left town with the quilt, do you?" Carmen suggested humorously, tinged with hysteria.

"Is that the latest rumor? Wouldn't *that* make things easier," Judy affirmed and grimaced. She thought for a minute about Carmen's comment. She had a missing quilt, a dead body and now a missing teacher.

"Who was the teacher?" she asked.

"Tom Lansdowne."

"Isn't he the judge I met yesterday?"

"Yes, that's right. I forgot you met him. I'm sure there's a good explanation, Judy. Probably some miscommunication," Carmen tried to wave off the situation.

"Yeah, probably," Judy agreed and dismissed the thought that was formulating in her head. "I hate to tell you this, Carm, but it's going to get worse. I have some bad news I have to talk to you, and the other women, about. Before it hits the newspaper. Let's go someplace quiet..."

Judy told Carmen about Gladys' death and then asked her to assemble the senior committee leaders so she could tell them the grim news.

"This is *terrible*," Rosemary exclaimed. 'Why would anyone want to kill Gladys? She wasn't the most popular person I've ever met but she never harmed anyone. Who could do this?"

Heads were shaking in disbelief around the small group.

Betty had joined the group late and the news had been repeated to her. "What a terrible, painful way to die," Betty exclaimed in an agitated voice. Judy looked at her steadily but said nothing. She hadn't yet told anyone how Gladys died. Feeling the scrutiny of the policewoman's gaze, Betty grew flustered. "I mean, you know, to be murdered and all." She waved her hand through the air as if to brush it all away from her.

"How did it happen?" someone asked.

"I can't say. It's still under investigation," Judy replied evenly.

"What are we going to tell people?" Rosemary asked with great concern. "Should we close the show?"

"I don't think that is necessary at all." Judy spoke without removing her gaze from Betty, trying to calm Rosemary down.

"Does this mean the quilt theft was connected to her death?" Angela asked.

"Well, it seems likely," Judy affirmed. "What good would it do someone to steal a prize–winning quilt?" she asked, finally breaking her study of Betty and looking around the group of quilters for ideas.

"It was a beautiful quilt," Betty was quick to compliment her deceased rival. Several heads nodded in agreement.

"Only if you just wanted it for yourself," Rosemary shrugged. "You certainly couldn't display it anywhere in town."

"But you could sell it somewhere out of town," Angela answered. "Where it was unknown."

"Gladys' quilt hadn't even been on display yet. Only a dozen people could have even see it," Carmen commented.

"The thief waited until after the judging was completed to steal the quilt, but before the Show opened, so for some reason whoever stole it didn't want the public to see it," Judy analyzed for them. "I'll need to talk to everyone who remembers seeing the quilt. Can you pass the word around, please?" Judy was using her official police voice and it was obvious this was an order.

"So, the question remains, did she steal the prize–winning quilt, or the quilt made by Gladys?" Angela commented.

"You're assuming that the killer was a woman," Judy pointed out, "and that the two events are connected, but there's no way to know, yet, that the same person committed both crimes."

"That would depend on whether the quilt was stolen before or after Gladys was killed, wouldn't it, Judy?" John asked. "If she, or he, killed Gladys before the quilt was taken, she, or he, wouldn't have known it was a prize–winner."

"You don't seriously think it was coincidental, do you?" Rosemary asked incredulously.

"Anything is possible," Judy shrugged. "By the way, what's this?" she asked as she pulled the round–bladed tool from her pocket.

"It's Gladys' rotary cutter," Betty replied. "Quilters use them to cut fabric to strip piece quilts. That was Gladys' specialty. She was one of the first in the Guild to do strip piecing. She ended up teaching everyone else."

"How do you know it belonged to Gladys?" Judy asked suspiciously.

Betty blushed and stammered, "The strip of fabric tied to the handle..."

"Everyone does that," Angela confirmed. "We tie distinctive ribbon or fabric to the handle, so we can tell whose is whose when we get together in classes or at metings."

"Why? Is it important?" Angela asked Judy.

"Would she have also used shears to cut fabric?" Judy continued, ignoring the question.

"Of course. You can do a lot with a rotary cutter, but you just can't do without a good pair of Hennkle shears," Betty continued, eager to be helpful.

Just then, Charlie, the day security guard, approached Judy to tell her Jeremy from the station had telephoned. She followed him to the security office and called in.

"Dr. Terrell just called. I thought you would want to know the results right away," Jeremy reported. He wasn't about to let another telephone message lapse.

Judy flipped open her notepad and said, "Shoot."

Jeremy read the report. Gladys had died at approximately nine to nine–thirty yesterday evening. Shears went straight through her heart. He had some further tests to conduct and would get back to her by tomorrow. She hung up the telephone and began humming while she thought.

Gladys had been murdered before the quilt was stolen, Judy pondered. That answered her first question about the quilt. So, if the thief and the killer were the same person, he or she had been after that particular quilt, by that particular quilt–maker, not the prize–winning quilt after all. Perhaps the fact that it won a top prize didn't matter to the killer, which made it all the more curious.

That eliminated one motive. But the question remained, why? What was so special about that quilt?

Back in the show hall, the news had now spread from the committee to the Guild members at large, and the vendors. Rumors were already flying. And conjecture ran rampant.

"Judy won't say how Gladys was killed!" Marion Cooper complained loudly.

"She was asking about her rotary cutter, though," someone offered suggestively.

"So, maybe the killer sliced her up into pieces..." Gerry Cooper intimated *sotto voce*, to muffled laughter, as he looked longingly and evilly toward his wife.

Picking up the gruesome theme, someone jocularly asked, "Do you suppose they used an Omnigrid cutting mat? After all, they are the best in the business!"

"Is that a commercial message?" Roberta Walker laughed.

Overhearing the comments, Candice Moore turned pale and walked away in disgust. "You're all being horrible!" she declared.

"The only person who disliked Gladys that much was Betty Harrison," Horace joked undeterred. "But nobody kills someone because they beat you out in a quilt competition!"

"At least she's being gracious about it all," Penny Prescott commented. Someone had mentioned how supportive Betty had suddenly become of Gladys and her quilt. Unlike her usual caustic rivalry that was often vociferously expressed.

"She can afford to be now. Who do you figure will win *next* year's quilt show?" Horace asked archly.

"Maybe it was one of the judges," someone joked. Wouldn't that be the unkindest cut, er, criticism of all!"

"It would make the *Guinness Book of Records* for having the last word, though!" Marion tittered.

Just then Betty passed near the *ad hoc* investigating committee of vendors.

"So, Betty!" Horace waved her over to the group. She approached smiling broadly, unaware of the conversation taking place. "You finally bumped off the competition, eh?" Horace called out jokingly to her as she drew near.

Betty's face went beet red and she flustered. Opening her mouth to speak, she was interrupted by Penny admonishing Horace's comment.

"That's a terrible thing to say, Horace! You should be ashamed of yourself! Look how embarrassing this is to Betty!" Then walking up to Betty, she took her arm and said, "Don't pay any attention to him! We know you must feel awful about this. No one really suspects you at all."

"Well, how could they," Betty replied, regaining her composure. "I was here all evening, with Carmen, Rosemary and Joan. I have plenty of unimpeachable witnesses. Do you?" she turned to face Horace. Everyone was now laughing at him.

"I don't need witnesses, dear. I have no motive," he threw back at her and flounced back to his booth where he had abandoned his wife, Jay, to a throng of customers.

Judy was busy asking official questions around the Show, piecing together details of everyone's movements on Wednesday. Angela remembered seeing Gladys leave the show around five o'clock. It was just before Charlie had locked up the back loading dock doors. All the vendors were present and registered and had moved their goods in. Anyone entering after that time would have had to use the front doors.

The big question remained. What did Gladys' quilt look like? In the end, eleven people could recall seeing it in detail. Four had been present in the hall just before it was locked up. Carmen, the Guild President; Rosemary, the Quilt Show Chairwoman; Joan, a Past President of the Guild; and Betty, the quilt hanging organizer. Three quilt hanging crew members also recalled it, and Susan, the Guild photographer. And, of course, the three judges, one of whom seemed to be missing.

Photographer? Ah ha! thought Judy. Maybe we'll get lucky! She asked Susan to bring her copies of all the photos she took of the set–up and the quilts.

At four o'clock Susan returned with the photos in an envelope, just as another call came in for Judy from Jeremy at the station. She took the envelope with her as she went to the security guard's office again to call in. Jeremy was extremely agitated.

"People are dying like flies in this town!" he exclaimed. Judy winced at the cliche. "There's been another murder!" he continued with rising excitement in his voice. She was going to have to do something about his unseemly emotional outbursts. He must have skipped the classes on professional detachment.

Judy told him to take deep breaths, calm down and give her the location details. Without telling anyone where she was going, she slipped out of the show and trotted to her squad car. Putting on the red flashers but no siren she sped to the address Jeremy had given her.

"What have we got here?" Judy asked the hotel manager as he unlocked the door and lead her into the room. The assistant manager had followed them down the hall and stood hovering at the door.

"Housekeeping found him a few minutes ago. We didn't touch anything," he explained, wringing his hands in agitation.

"Good," Judy grunted. She walked over to the man lying crumpled in a heap at the foot of the bed. There was a pool of blood all around his head and a deep indentation in the back of his skull. Hit from behind, he probably didn't feel a thing and went down like a stone, Judy observed. He was wearing a shirt unbuttoned at the neck and trousers. Socks, no shoes. His jacket and tie were lying on a chair. Judy picked up the jacket and quickly checked in the pockets. She found a wallet. Robbery was probably not the motive this time either, she thought. She was beginning to long for a simple robbery.

"You. Don't use that phone, but call an ambulance. Tell them, don't hurry," she commanded the assistant manager. "And here. Call Detective Schlosky at this number and tell him there's been a murder. He should send a squad car down." Schlosky was the Chief of Detectives for the homicide squad. She hated having to call them in again, but there would be recriminations if the murder scene was not properly investigated.

Judy surveyed the room. It looked like a typical executive class hotel room. Dark rosewood furniture, a king size bed with coordinated paisley–print bedspread and curtains. Tasteful but barren. Like all hotel rooms, everything was nailed down so it couldn't be removed without effort, or a screwdriver. Everything movable was monogrammed with the hotel logo, just to make sure no one would want to take it home. There was a small sofa and coffee table in one corner and a writing desk in the other.

The room was neat but lived in. It didn't look like it had been ransacked at all. The man had probably been there a couple of days. There were file folders scattered on the desk and an open briefcase sat on the credenza beside the television. A set of golf clubs in a golf bag sat propped in the corner. Businessman on a trip, brings his clubs to get in a few last rounds of the season, Judy observed.

"Name?"

"Mr. Tom Lansdowne," the manager read the name on the registration card that he had brought with him anticipating the police questions. Without being asked the next question, he offered. "He checked in on Wednesday. Supposed to leave Monday morning."

"No. What's *your* name?" she corrected.

"Eric. Eric Hampton."

"OK. Thanks, Eric. Tom Lansdowne. Now that's a familiar name," she mused out loud. Hmm, Judy thought. Here is Carmen's missing teacher. Now what did *he* have to do with all this, that got him murdered too?

Judy had to wait for the city homicide detectives to arrive. In the meantime she carefully went through the deceased's pockets, making notes on everything she found. There was a small brown walnutwood pipe, a well–worn leather pouch of tobacco, and a tool that pipe–smokers use to tamp down the tobacco and scrap out the bowl. When Judy held it in her hand it reminded her of her grandfather who smoked a pipe. She picked up the tobacco pouch again and zipped it open. Holding it to her nose, she sniffed deeply and the aroma wafted in a sweet memory of childhood when her 'Papa' had let her fill his pipe with the warm fragrant shreads and tamp them down. It had to be done just right. Too firm and the pipe wouldn't draw; too loose and it wouldn't stay lit. Judy smiled at the memory and replaced the items.

Along with the wallet, she found several business cards of people he had obviously met on this trip and various receipts for meals, and gas and incidental purchases.

The hotel manager stood politely but anxiously waiting for her to speak as she silently walked around the room. It was clear to him that she didn't want any interruptions.

Judy checked out the door. There was no sign of forced entry around the doorframe, so supposedly the killer had come in with him, or he had let the killer in sometime after his return. Judy noticed the room service tray that was sitting outside the door on the floor.

"When was this ordered, and delivered?" she demanded.

"I, um, I don't know," he stammered. He hadn't noticed it. "I can find out," he offered.

"Do so," she nodded.

There was only one snifter on the room service tray, so he hadn't been expecting anyone, Judy assessed.

She then interviewed the hotel staff for information about any unusual comings and goings of the deceased or his visitors. No one saw anything unusual. Even a phone call to the night auditor didn't reveal any clues. Someone would have to ride a horse through the lobby for anyone to think it was notable, Judy thought to herself. It's no wonder eyewitnesses at trials are so unreliable. People don't see half of what goes on around them.

She returned to the room just as the city squad car pulled up to the lobby. A minute later they entered the room.

"Tch, tch, tch. You're becoming very careless with your citizenry down here," the large detective admonished her sarcastically as he entered the hotelroom. "Schlosky tells me this is the second murder in two days. Keep this up and we'll have to open a branch office!"

Judy smiled wanly at his poor humor and said nothing. She found out long ago as a rookie officer that the best way to deflate any tormenter's enjoyment was to simply not bite on the bait. Don't let the bastards get to you, Mike used to say. Smiling and silence were her best allies.

Thinking an answer was different, of course. Jerk, she thought.

"You're Deputy Marshall, aren't you?" he grinned. "When you grow up are you going to be Marshall Marshall someday?" and he laughed at his own joke. It had probably taken him the whole car trip down here to come up with that witticism, she thought. She said nothing.

Unable to get a rise out of her, he sighed and grumped, "Gimme the stats." He flipped open his notepad, licked his pencil and prepared to write.

"Tom Lansdowne. Teacher in town for a conference. Last seen coming in by the night auditor yesterday evening shortly before ten. Ordered a bottle of cognac from room service at 9:55. About ten minutes later it was delivered. He didn't answer the door. Room service left the tray outside his door. Housekeeping found him an hour ago, at three o'clock."

He looked up at Judy. "Any probable?" he asked.

"Yeah, robbery," she suggested with a slight smile and narrowing her eyes as she spoke. He was looking down at his notepad and didn't see the look on her face.

"Any suspects or strangers seen entering or leaving the place?"

“It’s a hotel,” Judy commented sarcastically. “*Everyone’s* a stranger.”

The fingerprint man had followed the detective in and had been working his way around the room flicking a long–bristled brush embedded with fine powder around all the accessible surfaces, revealing dark smudges wherever there were fingerprints. In only a couple of minutes the room looked as if a demonic two year old with dirty hands had been set loose in the room. He had been silently moving around the room doing his job when, hearing Judy’s last remark, he started to softly sing, ‘People are strange, when you’re a stranger...’, a refrain from the Seventies hit by Jim Morrison and *The Doors*.

At least that made Judy smile. She caught his eye. He interrupted his refrain momentarily to say to her, “Five iron’s missing.” He kept moving, singing and flicking his fluffy revealing brush as he went. Like a fastidious housekeeper looking for tiny motes, he was hunting for latents.

“What’s that?” the detective asked over his shoulder.

“Five iron’s missing from the golf bag,” he repeated pointing with the handle of his brush. “From the look of his skull, it’s a possible murder weapon.”

“Killer had a bad slice, eh?” And the two men laughed heartily.

The ambulance took the corpse away to the county hospital morgue for another autopsy. When Darth Vader and the chimney sweep had left Judy went and washed her hands in the bathroom.

"Blech!" she said into the mirror, glad to be rid of them.

Before she left she carefully sealed the room with wide yellow plastic streamers that read, "Police Line. Do Not Cross" and walked away humming "Tie a Yellow Ribbon..."

Eight

Day three of the Quilt Show. Saturday.

The morning edition of The Banner hit the sidewalks with a heavier thud than usual. A late breaking story had screamed its way onto the front page. Naturally enough, news from the Quilt Show had continued to reach Brad Gilmour, the newspaper editor, who couldn't resist printing the serial scoops. It was a short article, though, in large type, because there were very few details to go on. Someone dug up an old photograph of Gladys and the newspaper photographer had taken a suitably dramatic picture of the empty display area. Mayor Brown got bumped off the front page.

A quilt had been stolen. The Best of Show quilt.

A body had been found murdered. The quilt–maker.

A teacher who had been one of the quilt judges had mysteriously disappeared and then turned up dead.

That's all that Clareville needed to read. By the time the Quilt Show opened at ten o'clock there was a long line–up at the door to get in. By noon all the special Show pins had been sold out, to morbid collectors who wanted a memento of the sensationalist Show. The raffle ticket ladies did a brisk business, too. The winner would have the dubious honor of possessing a quilt from a show where a quilter had been murdered.

It was a much busier day than the committee had planned. Good news for attendance. Bad news for reputation.

"This is no way to get people interested in quilting," someone in the line commented.

"I thought quilting was a non–contact sport!" was the reply.

"What are they going to do next time?" some wag asked.

Which sparked the inevitable tacky jokes. Someone suggested a new T–shirt: "Quilt 'til you're kilt".

It would be a hard act to follow.

Most of the idle gawkers went away unsatisfied. There was, after all, little to see. Just an empty display space with a small sign that read: "This quilt temporarily removed from the show".

Fortunately, most of the people who came to visit the Show were interested in viewing the quilts. Despite the mysterious crimes, the Clareville Quilt Show was a resounding success. There was a palpable air of excitement in the hall as quilters and quilt–lovers saw the variety and beauty of the quilts on view. Even though the Best of Show quilt was missing, there were still 199 other interesting quilts worth seeing.

The show must go on. Regardless of the voyeurism of the day, the conference and Quilt Show activities proceeded according to plan. The classes and demonstrations were conducted on schedule. With the exception of Tom Lansdowne's lectures.

At two o'clock in the afternoon there would be an auction of antique items. Most of the items were small, such as old thimbles and sewing boxes and hand–made lace. There was a much–admired and coveted beaded chatelaine with mother–of–pearl–handled scissors and sewing utensils that would probably sell for over two hundred dollars. A couple of old quilts were offered along with several antique quilt 'blocks' and quilt tops ready for quilting. Most of the items related to sewing or quilting, but not all. There was also a baby crib, a pram, an old spinning wheel, a rocking chair and a steamer trunk. All the items had been displayed on a raised platform throughout the show for previewing.

An hour before the auction started, Marion Cooper went over the auction items and along with two helpers, moved everything into order for the auctioneer who had arrived a half hour ago and was walking around the Quilt Show with his wife. Buyers had already started to assemble and had registered with the assistants in order to obtain a number with which they could bid. They were already staking their claim to chairs that had been set out in semi–circular rows around the auction podium.

"This is getting boring, you know," Marion declared in frustration as she briefly returned to her booth. "Everything is disappearing around this show."

"What's wrong?" her husband Gerry asked, as he waited on a customer, ringing in her purchase on the cash register.

"The key to the steamer trunk is missing from the auction. I know it was there yesterday. And I can't swear to it, but I believe it was there this morning. Now the trunk is closed and I can't get it open."

"Better go tell that police woman who's walking around the Show," he suggested sarcastically.

"I hope that's not connected to Gladys' death, too!" Marion shook her head. "It's not a bad idea though. Be right back."

"Where are you going *now*?" Gerry carped, annoyed that Marion was spending so much time flitting around the show instead of staying in their booth talking with customers.

"Aren't they trained to pick locks? I'll get Judy to open it," she said over her shoulder.

"You watch too much television! Besides, that's not what they're paid for!" Gerry called out to her back, but she was already gone.

"What's that all about?" Candice asked from her booth next door, having overheard some of Marion's exclamations.

"Oh, Marion can't find the key to the steamer trunk in the antique auction," Gerry replied casually, not looking up from the book he had returned to reading, between customers who had to interrupt him in order to pay for something. It's a wonder they ever sold anything given the lack of attention either of them paid to the public.

"Well, it's long gone by now," Candice remarked, muttering and fidgeting as she tidied up items on a display rack. "There's no point looking for it. Whoever is doing all this must be long gone by now. I don't know why everyone is going on and on about this!" she said in peevish exasperation.

"Wha?" He hadn't paid much attention to Candice's rambling outburst but his curiosity had been irritated. Just as Gerry looked up he saw a man had been silently standing in front of Candice's booth. He was looking directly at Candice but didn't say anything for several seconds and then moved on. Gerry thought it best to put his head back down quickly.

Hm, he thought. He'd heard rumors about Candice running around with some married man. He sniggered to himself. No wonder Candice seemed so on edge. Then he noticed she was wearing glasses today instead of her usual contact lenses. Surreptitiously studying her closer, Gerry decided that under the make–up her eyes looked red and puffy. She's still a fine looking woman, no doubt. The red hair might have been real once, but now it was probably dyed. A bit too brassy for my likes, he thought. But to each his own. Gerry shrugged and made a mental note to tell Marion about what he thought he saw.

Marion was a long time returning to the booth. Having found Rosemary, and then Judy, she complained about the lack of security in the building. Being the owner of "The Antique Attic" shop, Marion had offered to organize the charity auction in support of the Show. She had personally rounded up most of the donated items that were going to be auctioned shortly. It was more than annoying that someone's donation had been tampered with, even vandalized. It was downright embarrassing.

"It was here last night, I know," said Rosemary. "I walked the show before I left. In fact, John and I had stopped to comment on several of the items in the display. The trunk was standing open. I remember because it reminded me of one my aunt had when she came over from Europe after the War."

"Then where is the key now?" Marion demanded peevishly. "You're going to have to open it for me!" she commanded, turning to Judy.

"That's not her job," Rosemary objected, but Judy waved her off.

"Leave it with me," Judy requested. "I'll look into it."

Marion was not pleased but she left to return to her booth. An irritable woman at the best of times.

"Just what I need is another headache," Judy commented to Rosemary as Marion walked away.

"It never rains but it pours," Rosemary shrugged in reply. "What can I do to help?"

"You could go get Charlie," Judy suggested. "I don't have to time to look after it now. Maybe he can jimmy the lock open, if it's so important."

As it turned out, it was important. Charlie sat and played with the lock for ten minutes and finally fiddled it open. He and Rosemary lifted the lid, and inside, scrunched up in a mass of folds, was obviously a quilt.

"Oh, oh!" Rosemary exclaimed suddenly. "Don't touch anything!" she commanded pushing everyone back from the trunk. "Go get Judy quick!"

"Curiouser and curiouser," Charlie quoted from *Alice in Wonderland* as they waited for Judy to arrive.

A minute later she came jogging up to the auction display. Looking over the trunk without touching it, Judy hummed softly to herself. It was strains from *Leaving on a Jet Plane*: "All my bags are packed, I'm ready to go." Looks like it was packed in here in haste, she thought. The killer only had a couple of minutes from the time when the committee rehung the quilt until John locked the hall. She had to figure she could come back for the quilt later, and hasn't been able to. So someone is going to be pretty upset that we found this.

The killer has to know by now that we are looking for the quilt and couldn't risk approaching this trunk, Judy continued to analyze the situation. I could turn this whole hall upside down and I probably wouldn't find the key to the trunk. That would be far too easy to find the key on the suspect, too easy like television detective shows.

A small curious crowd had formed around the area. Word spread immediately through the hall and everyone who was free to leave their booth or committee station headed quickly for the back of the room.

"Don't touch the trunk," Judy directed, "but let's see what Gladys' quilt looks like." John had said the mystery woman who left the hall late Wednesday night had been wearing gloves, so Judy didn't expect to find any fingerprints. She just hated to have people meddling with her work.

They carefully extracted the quilt from the trunk and held it up, gently unfolding Gladys' last masterpiece.

"Is this a quilt *to die for*?" someone mockingly joked in bad taste. No one wanted to laugh out loud but several people snorted at the joke.

"You might as well hang this back in the show," Judy suggested. Let's see who salutes it, she thought to herself and stood back from the small crowd. Isn't the killer's face supposed to jump out at me in obvious guilt, Holmes? Judy beseeched her imaginary mentor, as she looked at the strangers' faces around her. She admired his uncanny ability to detect, with a single glance, a telling clue that enabled him to reconstruct not only the scene of the crime, but what the criminal had for breakfast! That was the advantage of being a fictional character who had access to the author's novel outline. Holmes was a train that had to run on a track to a predestined station. Life just isn't like that.

Who was the most interested in this quilt? she wondered.

Two white gloved ladies carried Gladys' quilt to the Best of Show display area and rehung it. Judy followed them.

"Are there any chairs around here?" she asked one of them.

"I'll get you one," she offered, and brought back a curved plastic chair.

Judy turned the chairback toward the quilt, just outside the cordoned area, straddled the chair and sat down, to contemplate the huge clue hanging in front of her.

"Tell me a story," she invoked the quilt. "What makes you different?" she asked it.

Judy sat for a long time, chin on hands, leaning against the back of the chair, lost in thought, humming the *William Tell Overture*, oblivious of the people who now came and went around her to view the prodigal quilt.

Now that Gladys' quilt was back on display, it was easy to see why it had won Best of Show. The quilt depicted a simple Autumn scene in the country. The trees were a riot of colors, all cut from a myriad number of different fabrics. Judy thought she recognized some of the cloth she saw in Gladys' workroom and felt a strange kinship to the woman, as if she had been part of the creative process in making the masterpiece. Having seen the workroom she felt privy to the quilt's inner meaning, if she could only decipher it. A good quilt will do that. It will draw you into itself. The more Judy looked at it, the more intrigued she was. I wonder how you do all this stitching, she mused and decided to find out more about quilt making.

In the scene, three young people were riding in an old convertible. The car was a cherry red 1957 Chevy. It was a distinctive car. The first year for the big rear fins.

There were two young women in the front seat. The woman driving was blonde and wore a bright flowery sundress. The other woman was holding a big sunhat down onto her auburn hair. They were laughing merrily. In the back seat was a handsome young man waving his arm. To one side, apparently out of sight of the riders, was a tree and behind it was a young girl in a pinafore peeking out at the car, as if spying mischievously on the trio. The car was travelling in a foreshortened landscape of bumps, hills and fields, and was headed toward a cliff and the seashore.

The more she looked at the quilt the more details Judy saw in it. In the background in the upper left corner, between two hills, was a simplified town. That's Clareville, she thought suddenly, as she recognized the double spires of the old Catholic church. In the upper right was another hill with a smaller stone church. From the front door of the church a miniature wedding party was erupting. And from the back door, pall–bearers were carrying out a coffin to the cemetery beside the church. Now that's weird, Judy thought, puzzled at the dark image imbedded in the otherwise pretty and gay quilt.

For some reason, Gladys' killer did not want anyone to see this quilt. Someone here had to be very nervous that it's been found. The quilt had to be telling a story that the killer didn't want known.

Judy was going to need help deciphering the message. It was time to round up a posse—of quilters.

With a start, Judy realized that she had been sitting in front of the quilt for almost two hours. She stood up and stretched. It was four o'clock. In her concentration, she hadn't even heard the noise and commotion of the auction as it took place. The quilt show would close for the day at six o'clock. Judy asked the committee chairwomen to join her at the quilt at six when they were free from their show responsibilities. They were likely to be the most knowledgeable about the quilt, and the quilter.

In the meantime, she wandered haphazardly through the quilt show. Judy decided she needed to know more about quilting if she was ever to understand this mystery. As she walked she overheard comments from quilters. She tried to look through their eyes as she listened. She heard remarks like:

"Look at all the details of the stitching here! I can't imagine how long this stippling took!"

"This is a beautiful piece of work, but it's machine–quilted. I prefer the traditional method, myself."

"I can't believe anyone could get that many stitches to the inch!"

"Haven't we seen a Sunbonnet Sue pattern at every show we have ever been to?"

"Applique is so difficult! I just don't have the patience!"

"Look at the way the colors blend together here. I wish I could pick out my fabric better!"

"Ah hah! A mistake! That makes me feel better! See, my quilt could have been in this show."

She stood for a few minutes in front of a particular quilt that caught her eye, studying it. At first, she didn't notice Angela walk up beside her. Angela noticed Judy frowning and said, "It can be a little overwhelming at times."

"Especially when you don't know what you're looking at," Judy sighed.

"Can I help you at all?" Angela offered. Judy looked at her closely for a minute and then decided she was intending to be genuinely helpful.

"That would be great," Judy said gratefully. "I'd like to understand more about quilting. I think it's important to this case. And I hate to admit my ignorance, but this is all new to me. I had a great–aunt who made quilts years ago, but I never paid much attention to it."

"That happens," Angela shrugged and smiled compassionately. "Sometimes we don't notice what is right under our noses. Let's walk around the show," she suggested.

For almost an hour, as they walked, Angela explained how a quilt is put together and all the sewing techniques that are required, and tried to give Judy a sense of why quilters spend their time and money quilting, especially since cheaper, more readily available alternatives are easy to find. Quilters love to share their love of quilting, hoping their enthusiasm will be infectious. It often is.

Basically a quilt is a fabric sandwich with a top, middle and bottom layers of material all stitched together with the 'quilting' stitches, either by sewing machine or by hand, she explained. It's as easy as that. And as complicated as that. What you do with the fundamental formula after that is up to your own creativity. The quilt can simply be a functional and practical bed covering, with minimal attention paid to making it attractive. Or conversely, it can be such a work of art that no one would dare sleep under it. And every stage in–between. There is a place for every quilt, and for every quilter, in that whole range.

That is part of the universal appeal—it's infinitely creative. Like painting, a quilter gets to use fabric like a giant paintbox and create anything they can imagine.

Beyond the function of the quilt, as practicality or artistry, there is the impetus for making a quilt in the first place. A quilter puts herself into her quilts. A quilt is an extension of the quilter's personality. It reaches out into metaphor. It's a symbol of her unique creativity. As simple or as complex, and as unique, as each individual.

Quilts are tactile, Angela went on to explain. In the often isolating and alienating high–tech world of today, the need for high–touch is intense. It is through art that we discover our humanity. Just as humans clothe and adorn their bodies in textiles, so too, do we clothe and celebrate our souls in textures.

It's no coincidence that the 'rule' in quilting is to only use 100% cotton fabrics. There are technical reasons for this. Cotton 'gives'; it's easy and forgiving to work with; it takes color reliably and faithfully. But more importantly, cotton is natural. It's a product of the earth and thus our quilts keep us grounded in nature.

Quilts are visual. If the eyes are the windows of the soul,

when you look upon a quilt, you have the opportunity to see the world through someone else's eyes. To see how they feel about form and color, and light and dark.

Quilts are a connection to the past. They come from our history and we pass them on to our future. So they are comforting and reassuring—that we are all part of a continuing cycle of life. That's why quilting is so often a communal activity. It would be hard to imagine creating something so comforting as a quilt in an environment other than one that is nurturing and supportive. Which is why guilds and quilting groups are so popular.

Quilting isn't a 'high art' or an accurate science. It takes very little 'talent' and yet a great deal of effort, making it an almost perfect Everyman handicraft. And above all, they are just plain fun to make.

For Judy, it was an enlightening tour, and in the end she was able to gain an appreciation for what all the fuss was about. The knowledge intrigued her even more.

Shortly after the show closed, again Judy sat straddling the chair looking at Gladys' quilt, this time surrounded by the Guild ladies.

"So, tell me about this quilt," Judy invited them.

"It's an applique quilt. Her own design," Angela pointed out and explained how an applique quilt is sewn.

"This is Clareville, right?" Judy pointed to some of the background details.

"Probably. Yes, it looks like it is," Rosemary affirmed.

"So is this a picture of Clareville?" Judy asked, waving her hand across the quilt.

"It could be," Carmen agreed. "Quilters often tell stories in their quilts. They're called 'memory quilts'. Popular these days. It's a way to tell a story about someone or something, or to leave a legacy behind."

"It could also be a map maybe. You know, like a road map or a treasure map leading to something. Did Gladys have anything valuable?" Joan suggested.

"This car," Judy pointed out, "is a 1957 Chevy convertible. It's a distinctive and somewhat rare car. My brother and I restored one once. It would be valuable. Did Gladys own one? I don't think so. There was no car in her driveway or garage," Judy said dubiously.

Heads shook, "No", or, "I don't know".

"Then why put it in the quilt, or the story?" Judy asked.

"Perhaps to set the story in a particular time and place," Rosemary suggested.

"1957," Carmen thought out loud. "Look at the fabric in the sundress, Joan. Wouldn't that be a Fifties print?" She leaned in closely to examine the material. Joan leaned in close to her.

"Yes, and the man's shirt could also be a Fifties," she affirmed.

"And the pinafore on the little girl is definitely a 50's or a reproduction print. I have some very similar to that in the shop," Angela pointed out.

"What does that mean?" Judy asked.

"Well, quilters like to make things as authentic as possible. So, when they make a memory quilt like this, they would use original fabrics whenever possible that would be consistent with the period they are depicting in the quilt," Joan explained.

"Where would she get fabric that old?" Judy asked surprised.

"Well, she might have bought it. You can still find lots of antique fabric around. Or she could have had it in her stash," Angela answered.

"Her stash?"

"Yeah, her stash of fabric. All quilters collect fabric. It's sort of a compulsion we have. You see something you like and buy it. You never know when you might need it or be able to use it in a quilt. You can always tell new quilters—they have no stash!"

"I see," Judy nodded, remembering the shelves of fabric in Gladys' sewingroom. There's a lot more to this quilting business than I thought, she realized.

"So you're saying this scene is actually set in the 1950's," Judy confirmed.

"It could be," said Angela. The quilters all nodded.

"This could be a story about her life, then, or something she remembered from the Fifties," Rosemary added.

"Who are these people then?" Judy asked.

Everyone studied the quilt in silence for several moments.

"Gladys was dark–haired when she was younger," Joan pointed out. "She could be the little girl in the scene. She's looking at the scene from a hiding place, behind the tree. Maybe this is something she saw as a child."

"Looks like a *menage a trois* in the car," Judy said pointing to the three figures. "Who are these people?"

"Whoever they are, if this is Gladys, and she is a little girl, then this was almost forty years ago! They would look very different today," Betty suggested.

"Anyone remember Gladys talking about something that happened to her forty years ago?" Judy prompted.

Heads shook. Shoulders shrugged.

"We're not much help, are we?" Carmen apologized.

"It's OK," Judy soothed her. "I didn't expect to have the answer jump out at us. But someone saw this quilt, and wanted to get rid of it. And maybe the quilter. Let's assume it's the mystery woman that John saw. She had to have seen the quilt, maybe by accident, sometime after two o'clock when Gladys arrived and the quilt was hung, until around seven when the judges started their rounds. Gladys went home at five. The killer left the show. Found Gladys at home. Killed her. Returned to the show. Hid somewhere. Waited and took the quilt down, hiding it in the trunk, planning to come back for it. You say there were only a few vendors still working on their booths after six thirty. So it was someone who came into the show in the afternoon." Judy was talking to herself and Holmes more than to her posse. She wanted to hear herself think out loud. It was a laborious process.

"She had to know she could come back into the show to retrieve the quilt. With impunity. Wearing either a vendor tag or a committee tag. She would have to be someone that no one would suspect, or recognize as a stranger, or in fact remember."

"You mean it's someone we know?" Carmen asked deeply concerned at the implication.

"Well, it seems everyone thinks I could have done it," Betty blubbered, turning red in the face despite her attempt at audacity.

"But you were with us all evening," Rosemary pointed out. "Judy said Gladys was killed between nine and ten. You were with us all along!"

"Except when we were leaving," Joan said thoughtfully, remembering. "You went back in to go to the washroom before we left. Remember?"

Betty started to stammer. 'Well, I didn't have time to take the quilt down," she exclaimed. "And I certainly didn't have time to go to Gladys' house."

Judy looked at her long and hard. The two women had disliked each other enough, she decided. She's been acting nervously. Maybe sometime Betty had wished Gladys was dead. Gladys turns up dead. Betty feels guilty. Probably just her conscience bothering her, and she dismissed the possibility.

"Nah," she waved it off. "Nobody kills someone because they beat you in a contest!" She smiled and the women all sighed with relief.

"Well, I'm glad you think so," Angela said.

"There would be a lot more dead quilters, if that were the case, I suspect!" Judy laughed. "OK. I guess that's all we can do tonight, ladies. Thanks for your help. You can head home now," Judy dismissed them. As an afterthought, she added, "Did Gladys have any close relatives? I'm having trouble locating any next of kin. Did she have any brothers or sisters?"

"Just one sister, but she died years ago. She rarely mentioned her," Rosemary replied.

"What was her name?"

"Pat, I think," Rosemary said again. "Is that significant?"

"OK, thanks. Good night!" Judy dismissed them without answering the question. She sat humming the refrain from the song 'Sisters' in *White Christmas* as she studied the quilt. "... Heaven help the mister who comes between me and my sister. And heaven help the sister who comes between me and my man..."

If Gladys is the little girl in thc quilt. Then the blonde woman in the car could be the blonde woman in the photograph, her sister Pat, and this scene happened forty years ago. There were no recent photos of Pat. I need to find out when the sister died, she reminded herself. That might tell me who these other people are. And that might tell me why Gladys was murdered, she decided.

Tom Lansdowne must have figured out what was in the quilt, and that got him killed.

Judy stood up finally and stretched. It was almost eight o'clock. She had some calls to make before the evening was through. The first would be to Brad Gilmour at The Banner.

Nine

The office of The Banner was located in a narrow store front on the old town square. Although the paper was printed at a modern production plant a few miles away, Editor and Publisher Brad Gilmour liked to maintain an office that was accessible to the public. Townsfolk could still hand their ad copy over the wooden counter and stop to gossip. Gossip often lead to stories, so he liked to be plugged into the local grapevine.

The newspaper had been printed continuously for seventy years and Brad was proud to carry on the tradition his grandfather had started. It was quite a tourist attraction. The tourists and children's bus tours loved to come in and handle the antique printing press that was on display along with framed front pages of memorable events that The Banner had covered. His grandfather's original quarter–cut oak rolltop desk was also on display with a teletype machine and an old upright 'Black Beauty' telephone. People liked to have their picture taken sitting at the desk.

Behind the old wooden counter, however, was the twenty–first century. When Brad took over the business, he installed the latest in database information technology. He was online to wire services around the world and through a modem was able to access everything short of top secret government files. For that he simply had to do it the old fashioned way and go through the usual channels—someone with inside knowledge and a desire to tell it. He called it his "HS&L system", an acronym for Hardware (the computer), Software (the information) and Liveware (the people). It rarely failed him.

It was after nine when Judy arrived at Brad's office and tapped lightly on the glass doors. He was waiting for her, smiled when he saw who it was, got up and ambled to the door. He locked it again after she entered. Brad's adolescent broad shoulders had shifted downward a long time ago and had come to rest around his sedentary middle–aged hips. He had become a pear–shaped wordsmith. His skinny photographer did all the legwork, running around town all day. For Brad the telephone was his umbilical cord to the outside world.

"Your call sounded important," he commented, with a question hanging in the air as they walked around behind the counter. Any call from Judy would be important to Brad. He would probably have written her long romantic love notes but unfortunately Judy wasn't connected to the electronic E–mail network. He could never find any comfortable face–to–face way of talking to her.

"It is. I need your help," she replied taking off her jacket and pushing the sleeves of her sweater up her arms. If Judy sensed his interest she never made any indication.

"The Quilt Show murders?" he asked perceptively, and hopefully. He wanted to flesh out the story for the next edition.

She nodded, yes, and explained about the quilt and finding Gladys' body. "I need to check the obituaries. Old ones."

Brad had sat down again at his desk. Judy sat in an old–fashioned wooden visitor's chair opposite him.

"Name?"

"Try Pat Brock," Judy suggested.

Brad quickly key–stroked the name in, pressed 'Enter' and a split second later, the screen flashed up the death announcement name and details from the archives. Judy whistled and shook her head at the speed of Brad's electronic magic box. His shrug said, 'Ah shucks, it's nothing'.

"When did she die?" Judy asked, flipping open her notepad.

"October 15, 1957," he read the screen. "Survived by one sister, Gladys," he continued to read. "Isn't that the woman who was killed the other day?" he asked.

Judy nodded yes.

"What's the connection?" he probed.

Judy ignored the question for the time being and asked him to read the rest of the screen. What else was there about Pat? He swivelled the monitor half around so she could also see it.

"Funeral services... da, da, da... here's something. She had just been engaged to be married the following spring. Sad stuff," he commented. "That's about it. Obits never usually tell you much."

"I know," she agreed, leaning over to see the screen and making note of the fiance's name.

Judy started to hum *Dead Man's Curve*, "Dead Man's Curve, it's no place to play", as she sat there thinking and tapping her pencil against the edge of her notepad.

"So, how does this fit in anywhere?" Brad probed again. "What does this have to do with Gladys' murder and the stolen quilt?" But Judy was still staring off into space, humming "Dead Man's Curve, you should stay away..."

"Earth to Judy!" said Brad, as he waved his hand in front of her. She focused back on him and he asked his questions again.

"We found the quilt today," Judy explained. "The Guild ladies seem to think it's some sort of 'memory quilt', they called it. It tells a story. Maybe of something that Gladys saw when she was a little girl. It might explain why someone would want to kill her. They didn't want anyone else to see what was on the quilt."

Judy showed Brad the photos of the quilt that Susan Patten had taken. He took out a photographer's magnifying glass and ran it over the picture.

"You think this is Gladys." He pointed to the little girl peeking out from behind the tree. Judy nodded.

"And this is probably her sister, Pat." She indicated the blonde woman in the car. "She was probably around eighteen or nineteen at the time. Just before she died. The guy in the backseat is probably the boyfriend. This is obviously Clareville." Judy pointed to the town in the background. It was had to distinguish the background detail in the small photograph.

"What's this?" Brad asked, indicating the small stone church in the other corner. "Looks like a wedding and a funeral on the same day. Some allusion to her going to be married, but dying first? Wait a second!" Brad smacked himself on the forehead. "I know this church! It's the St. John Parish Church out on Meadeway. And..." he turned back to the computer, clicked a button and checked the screen, "that's where Pat's funeral services were held! So, who's the other woman?"

"That," Judy sighed, "is the proverbial Sixty Four Thousand

Dollar Question."

"The murderer, you think?"

"Uh, huh," Judy nodded, deep in thought. "Do you know this car?"

"A '57 Chevy convertible," he answered.

"Right. 1957. So this is supposed to be the same year that Pat died," Judy observed. "She placed the quilt story right around the time Pat died. No, she placed it right on the *day* that Pat died. Look!" Judy exclaimed in excitement and pointed to the embroidered numbers on the license plate. It read 101557. "Ten fifteen fifty–seven. October 15, 1957! It looks like Gladys is telling us that the other woman in the quilt picture, was involved in Pat's death. And maybe the boyfriend too!"

Judy and Brad both looked up from the photo, at each other, wide–eyed with excitement like elated bloodhounds on the chase.

"What does your wizard brain there tell you about how Pat died?"

Brad keyed a couple of cross reference entries. Two or three screens came and went before him until he finally stopped on a microfiche of a newspaper front page story.

"Car crash."

"Bet the car was a..."

"Red '57 Chevy," he nodded.

"How?"

"Went off a cliff. Police suspected foul play. She'd been hit on the head before she went over, but they had no evidence to go on and the case was eventually closed, unsolved. Boyfriend was suspected briefly but he was cleared. Rumor was she picked up a hitch–hiker who probably killed her."

"Yeah, robbery again," Judy commented drily.

"What's that?" Brad asked but she waved away the offhand remark.

"This is no hitch–hiker. This is someone Gladys knew. Well enough to put a portrait of her in the quilt! Well enough to open the door to her house, and let her in!"

"A love triangle, perhaps?" Brad suggested.

"I think so. Gladys knew these people, or at least that this woman was going to be here at the Quilt Show," Judy concluded. "That's why she didn't want anyone to see the quilt beforehand. Maybe she didn't suspect the person would want to kill her. The statute of limitations has run out on Pat's murder, if it was murder, a long time ago. Gladys probably just wanted to embarrass the woman. Maybe drive her out of town. After forty years of keeping her secret, now she wanted to tell it. On the anniversary of her sister's death—October 15—the day the Quilt Show opened."

"There's a certain sense of closure to that," Brad nodded in admiration of the deceased quilter. "How are you going to find out who this other woman is?"

"Holmes will have to tell me," Judy answered.

"How's that again?"

"When you've eliminated all the possible answers, then the impossible, however improbable, is the answer."

"Right," Brad nodded. "Anything else I can do for you?" Brad blushed slightly at the unintended *double entendre* of the question.

"Not tonight. Thanks, Brad. I owe you one," Judy stood up and shook his hand firmly. She pushed the photographs back into the envelope and tucked it under her arm.

"Nada," he shrugged. "Just let me know the whodunit first."

"Mmm," Judy nodded noncommittally. Brad, as always had been unfailingly helpful, and she felt bad that she had let an important piece of the puzzle slip by him without drawing his attention to it.

Judy's next stop was back at the police station. Closed for the night, with the telephone switched over to the answering service, she had to unlock the door and let herself in. On her desk she found a note from Jeremy. Dr. Terrell had called in with his autopsy on Tom Lansdowne. Single blow to the back of the head at the base of the cranium. Spinal cord snapped at first cervical vertebrae. Death instantaneous. Wound consistent with the possibility of a golf club as the murder weapon. The blow had come from a horizontal angle, as if the club had been swung like a baseball bat.

There was nothing in the report that surprised Judy, so she turned her attention to her original and more pressing task. The second murder was undoubtedly connected to the first, albeit in a, well, secondary manner, she thought. Solve the first murder and the second one will solve itself, she decided.

She had some old police files to go through. Nowhere near as efficient as Brad's electronic information network, Judy had to rummage in banks of noisy metallic filing cabinets. But at least she had access to some inside information that would never have hit the streets. The original police investigation and photos of Pat's death.

She gathered up all the files and headed for home. It was near midnight, she noticed on the dashboard clock. No wonder I'm tired, she sighed, and thought longingly of her bed.

But something was telling her to keep moving forward on this case. Holmes was nagging her to have all the clues sorted out before the show ends.

Back home, Rufus was glad to see her. The wag–tail dog met her at the door. Whether from loneliness or the need to go out for a walk, she didn't know, but it didn't matter. It was nice to have someone to come home to, she thought, and made up her mind to get herself a dog, maybe something like Rufus. He was a shaggy in–between sort of dog, not too big, not too small. Too big to be cutsey, too small to be ferocious. Too wire–haired to be embarrassingly glamorous, too furry to be sleek. Just a warm, friendly, good natured mutt, happy to have a warm home. A dog that could appreciate a good woman.

They walked companionably in the cold night air. Rufus sniffed. Judy hummed 'How much is that doggy in the window?'

Back home again, in the kitchen, Judy put on a pot of real coffee for a treat, and while it brewed, she stripped down and put on a track suit and woolly socks. Taking a mug of steaming coffee, she retrieved the files and envelope of photographs from the front hall and went into the livingroom. She set the mug on a coaster and spread the photos out in sequence like tiles over the coffee table. The files and her notepad she set on the couch beside her. Before settling in to work, Judy got up, turned on the stereo low and slid in a cassette. She played Mozart, the string concertos. They always inspired her. Strings, she thought. How appropriate. Holmes played the violin. So she imagined him playing in the background to keep her company.

Judy sat back down on the sofa and closed her eyes. She pictured the banquet hall at the community center and the exhibition of quilts. In her mind she walked through the Show once more. Then she ran through the sequence of events.

Gladys spends weeks, or months, planning and making a surprise quilt without telling anyone. She plans the quilt to disclose the identity of the woman involved in her sister's death. On Wednesday, she arrives at the Show with her quilt. Quilt gets hung. Gladys leaves at five. Someone sees the quilt. Sometime around nine o'clock someone knocks on her door. She lets them in. Makes a pot of tea.

She expected the person. She expected to sit down and have a chat over a pot of tea. Things turn bad. Killer is provoked. Grabs shears and stabs Gladys. Gladys falls to floor, knocking over table and cups. Killer ransacks sewing room and removes evidence of the quilt. Killer then returns to Quilt Show. Because the judging is going on, the killer can't go near the quilt. She, or he, waits until everyone has left. The killer then quickly takes down the quilt and hides it in the steamer trunk, planning to return for it the next morning. Can't get near it for two days.

In the meantime, Tom Lansdowne has seen the quilt, and, on Thursday evening after we all left the show, he finally realizes what it means. He knows the identity of the killer. Killer comes to hotel room. A confrontation takes place. He gets clubbed with his own five iron. His body isn't discovered until Friday afternoon.

Saturday the quilt is found before the murderer has a chance to remove it. What is the killer going to do then? Nothing to attract suspicion. Like Elizabeth Taylor, they must be feeling like a cat on a hot tin roof. Or like a mouse whose tail is caught under the cat's paw. If she bolts, the cat pounces. If she stays put, it's only a matter of time until we find her.

Judy ran through the sequence twice more and then gave up thinking about it. Try another approach, Holmes tapped his violin bow on the table and goaded her. She looked at the police report and photos of Pat's death. The car wreck was not an unusual sight for Judy, but the battered body was still difficult to view unemotionally. She forced herself to just look at the facts and analyze them, not to think about the person who had been flesh and feeling so long ago. Pat was wearing a floral sundress. Judy picked up the quilt photo, looked at it under her hand magnifying glass, and smiled. The blonde woman in the car was wearing a sundress made from the exact same material as the sundress Pat was wearing at the time of the car crash.

"I'm impressed!" Judy whistled at the realization. Gladys had scraps in her 'stash' that included the original fabric from Pat's dress. Would she have inherited that from her mother perhaps, she wondered. Judy was amused by the possibility of 'heirloom' stashes being passed down from one generation of women to the next. Well, why not? she thought.

It was undeniable now that Gladys's quilt was telling the story of her sister Pat's death forty years ago.

She then picked up Susan's photographs of the Quilt Show set–up day one by one and started to simply describe to herself out loud what she saw in each one, without letting her prior knowledge of the theft or murder influence her observation, or interpretation. It was a technique she had learned to use to clear her mind, whenever the forest got in the way of the trees. She started with the early morning pictures and proceeded through the day. By the time she got to the six–thirty picture she was tired, and stopped to rub her eyes and stretch. Her monotone had put Rufus to sleep under the coffee table.

"OK. Just two more!" She pushed herself to finish the exercise. "Quilts all hanging on frames. In the background to the left, a chubby man in jeans and a sweater is working in one of the vendor booths. He's standing on a chair hanging a wicker wreath that someone hands him. The other person is partially obscured by the edge of the drape. Looks like another guy." Judy picked up her magnifying glass again to look closer.

"No. It's a woman! It's her!" she exclaimed suddenly to Rufus. The startled dog, jolted awake, whammed his head on the bottom of the table as he leapt to his feet.

"It's here, Rufus! John's mystery woman! Baseball hat and glasses! Why didn't I see this before! I'll bet if we get this photo enlarged and enhanced, that this turns out to be the woman John saw leaving the show! That's our quilt thief! And that's... our... killer!" She waved the photo triumphantly at the dog.

"Yes. Yes. Yes!" Judy read the name of the booth sign over the man's head in the picture.

"Well done!" Holmes applauded her, and she bowed her head

gracefully to her ever–present Muse.

Judy flipped through her notepad. She had taken down the names and addresses, date of birth and driver's license of every vendor as they had walked around the show.

She had the name. She tried to recall the woman's appearance at the Show. No wonder John didn't recognize her, she smiled. On the set–up day she probably wasn't wearing any make–up, had her hair under the cap and wore glasses. But on the show days she had her hair and face done. And wore contact lenses. Simple and innocent enough changes normally, and enough to confuse any male eyewitness.

He didn't see her hair. He would have remembered that.

It was red.

Just like the woman in the car in the scene in Gladys' quilt. This was the woman Gladys wanted everyone to know was linked to her sister's death. How? Was she in the car the day Pat died? Judy checked the old police report again. The autopsy indicated the woman had been hit on the head and was dead before the car went over the cliff. And what about the boyfriend? Had he been there, too? Why did Gladys put him in the picture in the quilt? Was she implying he was involved, too? The report said that he had been questioned afterward but had a substantiated alibi so he was dismissed. The case was closed as a suspicious car crash.

Judy leaned back on the couch, looking at the photo still in her hand. So, we know who you are, she thought.

Now, we have to prove it.

Ten

Sunday morning was the last day of Clareville's sensational Quilt Show. There were shorter hours on the Sunday. The Show was only open from noon to five.

Sundays are always quieter at quilt shows. Everyone sleeps late, goes to church or brunch, and takes a relaxed approach to any excursions they make in the day. There are more families at the show, dressed up. It's an outing for them. Fewer serious quilters. The serious quilters have been living in the fast lane for three days, are exhausted and ready to go home.

The fact that the missing quilt had been returned to the Show didn't cause nearly as much stir as the disappearance had. Attendance would be low and sporadic. By four o'clock most of the vendors will be anxious to go home.

A loud ringing woke Judy up before seven o'clock. It had been well past two in the morning when she went to bed and Judy was a woman who really needed her sleep. She automatically reached out for the alarm. But it didn't stop. Then she groggily realized it was the telephone that was ringing.

"Hello," she whispered into the mouthpiece. Her mouth was dry and sticky. "This better be good," she grumped into the phone.

"Hello? Judy?" said the voice on the other end. "It's Doctor Terrell."

The coroner. What's he doing calling me on Sunday morning,

Judy thought trying to rouse her tardy brain.

"Sounds like I woke you up. Sorry. But I thought you might want to hear the results of the autopsy right away."

"Hn, huh," she mumbled. "Shoot." She reached for the pen and paper on her nightstand. There was a half empty glass of cola watered down by melted ice cubes left from last night, or it could have been the night before. She took a swig and swished her mouth with the ersatz mouthwash.

"Well, this is really interesting," he started. "I can't say I've ever seen anything quite like this before..."

"Cut to the chase, doc," Judy said irritably. "Gladys was stabbed. What can you add?"

"She was stabbed alright. Trouble is she was also poisoned!" He stopped to let the fact sink in. A moment passed. A very long moment.

"What do you mean she was poisoned?" Judy exploded, suddenly wide awake. "How much deader do you need to get than dead!"

"I know, I know! It sounds impossible! When I first looked at the body I knew she had died of hemhorraging due to the thoracic stab wound. But there was something odd about the discoloration of the extremities. It didn't seem right, so I sent off some blood tests. She had been poisoned some time before she was stabbed."

"With what?" Judy automatically asked.

"Do you know any Latin?" he asked.

"No."

"Then why ask? It's a long name that no one can spell. Your

killer had to know something about chemistry. It's a slow acting poison at that. Someone really must have hated this woman. They wanted her to die a slow, and ultimately painful death," Terrell explained.

Judy took careful notes as he described the chemistry of the poison and its derivation from a common garden-variety plant.

Judy whistled. "Boy, if people only knew what they could cook up from their backyards..."

"How was it administered?" Judy then asked.

"Ingested. Probably in something she drank."

"Like hot tea with sugar?" Judy suggested, remembering the half full teapot in Gladys' kitchen.

"Yes. That would work. It's a dark brown liquid, only slightly bitter, so sweet tea could disguise the taste. But the killer must have grown anxious that she wasn't dying fast enough, or maybe Gladys started to suspect something was wrong, and so he, she, or they had to stab her." The doctor was trying to fill in his own conjecture.

Judy's head was swimming with the new information.

"I *know* who killed her! At least, I know who stabbed her," she said. "When was the poison administered?" she asked, trying to piece together what she knew about everyone else's whereabouts on Wednesday evening.

"Probably around six o'clock in the evening. The meal she ate delayed absorption. She wouldn't have started to feel anything for several hours."

"So someone could have gone to her house, sat down for a friendly cup of tea, poisoned her and then returned to the Quilt Show.

Or been anywhere where they were innocently observed and without an opportunity to stab her which took place later," Judy said, thinking out loud.

"That's possible," he confirmed. "Does this mean you've been looking for the wrong person?"

"No. It just means someone else also had a motive to want her dead."

"It's ironic though, you know. That's not all I found, Judy," the coroner continued.

"Don't tell me she was also strangled!"

"No. No, not that. It's ironic, because they didn't need to kill her. She had cancer," he explained. "Advanced ovarian cancer."

"No shit!" Judy exclaimed.

"Fairly common unfortunately. Gladys was, what, fifty years old, unmarried, no children?"

"Forty-eight," Judy corrected.

"Highest incidence of ovarian cancer is women in their late forties, never having given birth. Something to do with the hormone factors..."

"So she was going to die anyway," Judy interrupted. "When? Can you tell?"

"Could have been two months, or a year. Hard to say what makes one person survive longer than others. It was advanced, and inoperable."

"Would she have known?"

"I'm pretty sure she did. There were abdominal scars. Recent. Probably exploratory surgery. She must have known. She would have been in some pain."

Judy was quiet for a minute while she thought, then said, "I'm sure she knew, doc. That's why she made the quilt. She had to tell someone before she died," Judy mused out loud.

"What quilt?" the doctor asked. "Oh, you mean the one that was stolen from the Show?"

"Yes. But it's been found again. Thanks for calling. You were right. I needed to know this."

"It sure beats all, doesn't it, Judy? It's ironic. A woman's going to die anyway and one person kills her and another tries to. Why were they so mad at her? Who was she?"

"She was a quilter," Judy replied evenly.

"Didn't they know that all they had to do was wait?"

"Someone *will* be waiting," Judy said affirmatively. "In jail."

"With all that time on their hands, maybe your killer can make a quilt," Dr. Terrell tried to make a joke.

Judy hung up the telephone and flopped back onto her pillows. The new information was buzzing around in her head. The poisoner must think she's literally gotten away with murder, she mused. As soon as she found out Gladys had been stabbed, she figured she was off the hook because we'd be looking for the scissor–wielding killer. Someone's walking around feeling pretty sure of themselves. And I know who that would be, Judy decided, picked up the telephone and dialled Jeremy's home number.

"Hello?" squeaked a voice at the end of the line. He sounded as fuzzy–headed as Judy had been minutes previously.

"Jeremy? Judy. Sorry to wake you, but there's something I

need you to do."

She gave him instructions to obtain a search warrant from Judge Kaufmann. He was to meet her at the address at twelve o'clock. She had something to do in the meantime.

It's a crazy world, she thought and laughed out loud. Everything had fallen into place finally. All she had to do was prove it. Then she got up and went to the shower. As the warm water pummelled her, she sang out loud, full throttle and off-key, 'I Got You Babe', changing the words as she went.

"They say we're dumb and we don't know/

"Cops find out, even though we're kinda slow..."

Within minutes she had dressed—in a crisply ironed uniform today, it would be an official day, to be sure. She even took time to give her black shoes an extra shine. Over a microwaved muffin and coffee, Judy told Rufus where she was going. He looked eager to accompany her on the case, as if he could be helpful, so Judy had to explain why he couldn't go with her. He listened patiently, watching her with knowing brown eyes, then went to lie down dejectedly on his bed by the back door. "Next time, buddy," she promised as she patted him goodbye. The one single wag of his tail said, 'You say it but you don't mean it'.

The first thing Judy did was drive over to the hotel where yesterday's murder had occurred. She had a hunch the murderer was operating in a state of panic and may have dropped the murder weapon in the vicinity. She was hoping that would be the case. "It would be nice if just one thing was simple and straightforward," she said to herself.

"Sometimes the obvious is the answer," Holmes said to her. Judy was standing in the middle of the Tom Lansdowne's hotel room.

"Now, I'm the killer," she said out loud. "What do I do?"

She stood beside the chalk outline on the carpet.

"We're arguing. I haven't brought any weapon with me. I reach out." Then pretending to hold a club in her hand she swung at an invisible victim.

"He crumples at my feet. 'Oh my God, I've killed him!' I say and run out."

Judy went to the door, entered the hallway and closed the door behind her. She looked up and down the hall.

"Maybe I hear the elevator coming. Someone may see me! I run the other way." Judy went to the emergency staircase at the end of the hall, opened the door and started walking down the stairs. The room was on the tenth floor so it was unlikely to be the kind of staircase that people would use often. On the landing below she found what she was looking for, the bloody golf club.

"Bingo," she said pulling a green garbage bag from her pocket and carefully picking up the club with the plastic so not to disturb any fingerprints.

At eleven o'clock Judy pulled up in her squad car to a little brick house in an older part of town. There were two large Maple trees on either side of the path that ran up the middle of the small front yard. The trees had clearly outgrown the yard. Piles of fallen leaves on one half of the lawn indicated that someone had been raking the diminutive greenspace recently. There were yellow and rust colored chrysanthemums growing in neatly trimmed gardens and in dozens of terracotta pots on the front porch. Judy smiled when she saw the cheerful flowers and bent over to pluck off a single bronze bloom which she twirled between her thumb and forefinger as she stepped up to the porch. Two small economy cars were parked in the narrow concrete driveway. Someone would be home. Judy rang the bell and waited. She caught a whiff of the fresh October smell of burning leaves. She was just about to reach and ring the bell again when someone spoke behind her.

"Hello?" called a short grey-haired man carrying an empty bushel basket. Startled by his voice, Judy wheeled around as she pushed the flower into her jacket pocket. He had evidently walked up the side of the house and come up around the porch to the front yard. "Can I help you, officer?" he asked putting the bucket down.

"Are you Mr. Harrison?" Judy asked, walking down the four steps to the front walk. "I'm looking for your wife. Is she home?"

"Yes, I'm Albert Harrison," he nodded. "She's in the backyard. We're doing some yard work today. Oh, well, I guess that obvious," he tittered and indicated that Judy should follow him by pulling off one of his oversize canvas gardening gloves and waving it toward the side walkway that lead to the backyard. Judy followed him.

"You have some lovely mums in your garden," Judy complimented him as they walked. "You must enjoy gardening." She was uncomfortable making idle pleasant conversation but he didn't seem to notice.

"It's really my wife who does it all. She just loves her mums.

Every years she plants 'em and nurses 'em. I just lift and tote," he laughed.

As they reached the fenced–in backyard, Judy saw a small fire smudging in the far corner of the yard. A woman in a thick padded jacket and toque was bending over a flower bed with a trowel in her hand.

"Here she is. Dear, this police officer is here to see you." She straightened up suddenly when she heard her husband's voice, and turned around with a surprised look on her face.

"Oh, hello Officer Marshall. It's nice to see you, again. Is there something I can do for you? What brings you to Washburn Avenue?" she smiled, and stepped out of the garden, coming toward Judy.

"I want to talk to you about Gladys Brock,' Judy explained and watched for the woman's reaction. There was an almost imperceptible faltering in her step and then she stopped, looking down as she carefully removed her gardening gloves one finger at a time. She removed them as if they were skintight. With loose fitting garden gloves you simply grab the floppy fingers and pull.

"Oh, that terrible mess at the Quilt Show," Albert interjected in the meantime. "Tch, tch. Such an awful thing to happen."

"Yes, it was," the woman said calmly. "Thank you Albert. You can finish up in the front yard while I talk to Miss Marshall."

She was clearly dismissing her husband, who mumbled, "OK, dear," and ambled away.

Turning to Judy and lapsing into familiarity, she said, "Now, what can I do for you, Judy?" She walked casually over to a wooden picnic table and sat down on the end of the bench, placing the gloves on the table beside her. "I thought I had already told everything I know about the missing, and then not–missing, quilt." She pulled off the toque and loosened her hair with her fingers.

"There's been a new development. I thought you might be able to shed some light on it for me," Judy explained as she also walked to the picnic table and sat down facing the woman, watching her closely from behind her dark glasses. "It seems that Gladys had two visitors on the night she died."

"Oh?"

"Yes. You see, we know Gladys died at around nine thirty from a stab by a pair of scissors. That was about the time you were at the judging of the quilts."

"Yes, that's right, I was," she nodded.

"Sometime before then, say, around six o'clock in the evening, after the quilts had been hung and everyone went home for dinner, someone else paid Gladys a visit and put poison in her tea."

"No! Really?" The woman fiddled with the gloves on the table in front of her, folding and unfolding the fingers one by one, then picking one up and putting it on again. Judy noticed her hands trembled slightly despite the distraction of the nervous activity.

"Yes, really! It was a rare, slow–acting poison. Derived from special plants," Judy said slowly.

"Who could possibly have done that, do you suppose?" She sat squeezing the empty fingertips of the gloved hand.

"There was no sign of a forced entry. I figure it was someone who knew Gladys well. Well enough that she would invite her in and offer her a cup of tea. Someone who knew her well enough to know that Gladys always drank tea with sugar, which would disguise the bitter taste of the poison. But it was someone who hated Gladys enough to want to kill her. Someone who wanted her to die a slow and painful death, in retribution for the years of torment and humiliation the killer had suffered. Someone with a long memory and an axe to grind. Someone who saw Gladys' last quilt as the final straw, and snapped."

"Now Judy, Gladys couldn't possibly have had an enemy like that, could she?" she asserted, and laughed nervously.

"It doesn't sound familiar to you at all? So, you can't think of anyone who might fit that description?" Judy coaxed.

"Someone would have to be crazy to do that."

"Crazy yes. And lucky, too."

"What do you mean?" she stammered.

"Lucky, because if the poison had worked its course, Gladys would have died sometime after midnight. Instead she was still alive at nine–thirty to answer the doorbell again. She probably wasn't feeling too good by then. Maybe a headache and a little queasy. But she was still well enough to get into a disagreement with the second visitor, who picked up a pair of shears in a fit of anger, and stabbed her!"

Judy put her hand into her jacket pocket and extracted the rusty blossom. Leaning her elbows on the table, she idly twirled it between her fingers in front of her face. The woman stared at the hypnotizing flower, her eyes widening in surprise, or fear.

"Lucky, because the coroner's report and the official police report will state that Gladys died from the stab wound to the heart. You can't try two people for the same murder," Judy concluded.

"What are you going to do about it?" she asked softly.

"I figure it was an opportune crime of passion by someone consumed with jealousy. It seems Gladys was fated to die anyway for other reasons. It probably wouldn't serve any purpose in pursuing the other attempted murderer. It isn't the sort of thing that is ever likely to happen again, *is* it?" Judy said firmly.

The woman shook her head and said in a barely perceptible voice, "No, I wouldn't think so."

"I thought not." With an elaborate gesture, Judy put the flower carefully back into her pocket and patted it securely, saying, "Thanks for your help today."

Then she slowly removed her aviator glasses, folded them precisely and put them in her breast pocket, while the woman sat rigidly controlling her tremors. Judy looked her straight in the eye and said carefully, "I'll be seeing you around, Betty."

Then she stood up and walked away without looking back.

As Judy passed through the front yard, Albert stopped his raking and waved cheerily goodbye.

"Next year, try geraniums!" Judy called as she slid into her car. She smiled to herself as she saw Albert in the rearview mirror, scratching his head in puzzlement.

At five to twelve, Judy pulled up to the large suburban bungalow on the quiet cul–de–sac. Jeremy was already waiting there for her. He was nervously pacing up and down the sidewalk, but there was no squad car on the street.

"Where did you park?" Judy asked as she got out of the car. "You didn't need to hide the car, you know."

"Um. I didn't. Um." Jeremy was almost agitating himself out of his uniform. Judy crossed her arms and leaned her bum against the front fender of the car waiting for his answer. He took a deep breath and said in a rush. "I locked the keys in the trunk of the squad car. I was checking the equipment and set them down. I didn't mean to do it. I know I'm a klutz!"

Judy just laughed. "Oh, Junior, what are we going to do with you?" She sighed in mock exasperation. "Then how did you get here?"

"Took a taxi. I won't put in an expense chit for it!"

Judy just laughed again and shook her head. "Did you at least bring the warrant?"

"Yes. I have the warrant, but I don't think anyone is home," he pointed out. The driveway was empty. The garage door was open and there was no car inside.

"I wasn't expecting anyone home," Judy said.

Jeremy looked puzzled. "I want to look around, not talk to anyone," she explained.

They walked up to the front door and rang the bell.

"Just in case," Judy shrugged to Jeremy. Two more rings. No answer. She motioned him to follow her around the side of the building. There was a flagstone path that lead to a patio with double French doors. The yard was sequestered with a high fence all around and tall trees that obstructed any view from neighboring houses. The more money people have, the less they want their neighbors to see what they have, Judy mused.

"These will do," she said to the doors, and pulled a small leather packet from her inside breast pocket. She flipped it open and revealed several long slender shiny steel instruments. Looking at the doorknob, she selected one and bent down to eyeball the lock. Slipping the steel into the lock, she manouevered it around slightly, turned the knob, and the door opened.

"Where did you learn to do that?" Jeremy whistled in admiration.

"My brother," she replied.

"What was he, a second storey man before he became a cop?"

"No. When we were kids we used to pick every lock we could find. There wasn't a lock we couldn't open. It was sort of a competition we had. Maybe that's why we both became cops."

Judy put the steel back in its slot and flipped the leather closed. Hefting it in her hand she said, "I tell you, what I wouldn't have given to have a set of these back then! We were using bent hairpins and coathangers."

Jeremy laughed. It was the first time Judy had ever shared anything about her past, or private life, with him. She was finally starting to warm up to him, he felt. Maybe there was hope for them yet. Now if he could just solve Sheriff Burnet and get into his good books.

They entered the house and closed the patio doors behind them. "What are we looking for?" he asked as they moved quietly through the sun room.

"Murder One, two counts," Judy replied. She called out loudly to make sure no one was home and then they proceeded to carefully search the whole premises.

A few minutes later they were working their way down the central hallway, room by room. Judy entered the bedroom first and Jeremy followed her in. She motioned him to check the closet and she moved to the chest–high dresser, examining each drawer from the bottom to top. When she saw the top of the dresser she stopped in her tracks and whistled softly. Jeremy thought it was a signal and came up behind her.

"What have you got?" he asked.

Judy didn't answer. She just sat down on the bed and started humming "You ougtta be in pictures", as she sat rubbing her chin with her hand, studying the dresser. Jeremy stood looking, but he didn't know at what. She sat for several minutes in contemplation, getting up once to look closely at, but without touching, the items on the dresser.

Finally Judy said, "We have to take some fingerprints."

"We don't have the kit to do that," he protested.

"Didn't they teach you anything about fingerprinting at the academy?"

"Of course, we learned how to use the fingerprinting equipment issued by the force in its correct and lawful manner," Jeremy replied in his best official tone.

"Hell, we don't have time for that," said Judy. "We have to improvise. All we need is some powder and a brush. And some sticky tape. See if you can find some tape in the desk or the kitchen. And bring a plastic baggy from the kitchen," she called after him.

In the meantime, Judy went around the bed to the other side of the room where a woman's make–up table stood. It was the old–fashioned kind that had a small kneehole where you sit in front of a large round mirror. There were two files of small drawers that ran down each side of the kneehole. Dozens of tubes of lipstick and liquid make–up, hair brushes and eyebrow pencils lay scattered over the table top. Opening the drawers, she found a small oval box of dusting powder. Inside the box was a fluffy pink powderpuff. She shook it gently and sneezed as the cloud of heavily perfumed powder hit her nose.

"Good enough," she said, just as Jeremy returned. "OK. This is what we do," Judy said, moving back to the dresser, and fluffing the powder around. She smiled at the unasked question on his face. "You learn this in the academy cafeteria, not in the classroom," she explained.

"Now use the tape to lift up the print. Right there. See? Good. Fold it over to seal the tape. Label it," she directed as she handed him a pen.

Judy went to the make–up table, picked up a pair of tweezers and used them to pick up a single item from the dresser and drop it into the plastic baggy.

"Now we need a full set of prints. Where's the best place to get that, do you suppose?" she mused.

"The bathroom," Jeremy suggested. "The drinking glass."

"Good idea!" Judy snapped her fingers. She was almost giddy with the excitement of the chase she was on. They went to the bathroom and carefully extracted several prints from the glass.

"Now, we have to make one quick trip to the hotel," Judy said.

"Where that fellow was killed Friday night? Why?"

"We need a set of his fingerprints, too. We'll try *his* bathroom waterglass," she smiled at Jeremy and patted his shoulder.

After removing a set of prints from the waterglass in Tom Lansdowne's hotelroom, Judy headed downtown in the squad car.

"Where are we going now?" Jeremy asked.

"To The Banner. We have to catch a killer this afternoon," she smiled.

When they pulled up, Brad was just opening the front door.

"Good timing!" Judy called as they climbed out of the car. "Thanks for coming over, Brad. I need your help again."

"More obits?" he asked as they all entered the office. Brad walked over and turned on the lights. "Somebody else die?"

"No. We need to use your darkroom."

"This way." He gestured them toward the back of the long narrow office. Behind the wooden front counter were two modern desks. One paperless surface contained Brad's pristine electronic wizardry. The other was littered with papers, files, contact sheets, post–it notes and empty film containers. It was Felix and Oscar go to the office. Behind the two desk spaces were five foot freestanding room dividers that camouflaged the mess of boxes, filing cabinets and coffee machine. And beyond that was a door with a red light over it. The dark room. Luther's darkroom. Judy was surprised to see that it was immaculate. Everything else about Luther was chaotic, but this all–important laboratory was free of clutter. This was where the real Luther lived.

"He'll kill me if he finds out I let you in here," Brad said. Even though he owned the newspaper, he could be intimidated by his skinny employee newsman–photographer. After all, what would the paper be without pictures. Brad was the endomorphic deskman; Luther was his ectomorphic legman.

"We won't leave any fingerprints," Judy joked. She was feeling almost light–headed with the excitement of the case. Especially now that she had solved the bizarre set of circumstances.

She showed Brad and Jeremy what she needed done. They had to use the enlarger that is used in making negatives to blow up the fingerprints that she and Jeremy had removed earlier. They exposed the prints directly onto photographic paper and within minutes she had eight by ten enlargements of all the fingerprints, appropriately labelled.

"Now we'll see what we've got," Judy said as they pinned the wet prints up on lines strung across the room for drying. The fingerprints were faint and broken in spots due to the non–professional powder but there was enough to make comparisons.

Judy smiled with satisfaction.

She was sure she had the murderer now.

Eleven

The last hour of a quilt show is always tough on the vendors and committee. Almost everyone has gone home, except for a few last–minute shoppers and gawkers. The gypsies are ready to pack their tents and steal silently into the sunset toward their next oasis. Its the soup bone end of the feast.

The classes have all ended and the students have lugged their sewing machines home. The quilt hanging crew has returned and are milling idly around the hall, waiting to reverse the process they so carefully executed four days ago. The local quilters are anxious to retrieve the quilts they have on display, and the committee is tired from all the long hours they put in at the show, before the show, after the show. Everyone will want to sleep in late tomorrow, but few will be able to. Tomorrow is Monday and everyone returns to their regularly scheduled lives.

At four o'clock the last flurry of excitement for the weekend took place at the raffle quilt drawing. A gaggle of opitimistic ticket-holders stayed around the hall, hoping to be present when their name was called. It almost never happens that way.

At four–thirty, the vendors had started to surreptitiously pack their goods away. It is always show policy that no booth is dismantled until the official close of the show. But everyone subtlely breaks the rule by putting away a few things here, a few things there, in order to save a few precious minutes time when the break–down comes. They also do 'the vendor shuffle', where all the vendors go visiting each other and picking up any bargains they need for themselves. It helps fill the time as they wait for the close of business.

At a quarter to five, Judy strode purposefully into the Community Center with a large brown envelope tucked under her arm. Jeremy followed at her heels. It's always a terrifying sight when two police officers in full uniform march determinedly into a room.

The ladies at the registration table scurried inside when they saw the police coming.

Judy had telephoned John and asked him to meet her there. He was waiting at the front door and she paused to greet him and give him instructions.

The invisible telegraph had instantaneously electrified the almost– empty banquet hall. Carmen came toward the front of the hall and met Judy as she walked in. Judy spoke to her briefly and Carmen fell into step behind them as they strode to the vendors' booths. At first everyone else tried to act nonchalant and kept their distance from the police presence, in case it was headed toward *them*. It's curious that even innocent people start to feel guilty around official uniforms.

Judy walked up to a woman who was bending over packing sachets of pot pourri into a cardboard box. She looked up in surprise.

"I'm here to talk to you about your involvement in this case of the missing quilt," Judy said taking off her sunglasses.

"I don't know what you're talking about," she replied with an attempted smile. "I already told you everything I know."

"Accompany us to the display area, please," Judy said without smiling. It wasn't an invitation. It was an order.

Judy marched to the back of the hall. The woman followed and Jeremy fell in behind to make sure she kept up. Like the Pied Piper they started to gather a small platoon of onlookers trailing after them. Whispers were passing behind hands.

Judy came to a halt at Gladys' quilt and spun around to face the troop behind her. Ignoring the crowd and looking only at the woman, she said, "I believe that you stole this quilt on the eve of the Quilt Show. And I can prove it."

Judy took the envelope from under her arm. She pulled out a photograph and handed it to John.

"John, would you please look at this photo and tell me what you see in the circled area."

John took the photo and squinted at it. "There's a woman wearing glasses and a baseball cap." He paused. "Wait a second! It's the woman I saw leaving the hall after the committee had left on Wednesday night, the night the quilt was stolen!" he said in surprise, looking up and down from the photo to the woman.

"Thank you." Judy took the photo and handed it to the woman. "Is this not your booth? And is this not you on Wednesday evening, setting up your booth?"

"Yes. But that doesn't mean anything," she replied testily.

"You were the only person in the hall after the quilt was rehung by the committee members. It means you had the opportunity to take down and hide the quilt, hoping to return for it at a later time," Judy explained.

"Why would I do that? Besides, the quilt has been found, so what?" she shrugged.

"Why, indeed? Because you didn't want anyone to see this quilt. Because you were afraid that someone would understand what the scene in the quilt depicted and you would be ruined. You see, this is a 'memory quilt'. It's a kind of quilt that tells a story. It tells a story that Gladys Brock wanted to tell and had waited for forty years to tell it. It's something she saw as a little girl and was probably too scared ever to tell anyone that she saw it. You see, she saw her sister, Pat, being killed, and pushed over a cliff in her car. A car just like the one in the quilt. A red '57 Chevy convertible."

With that, several hands in the crowd pointed to the quilt and heads started to nod as neighbors made quiet comments to each other.

"And she knew why," Judy continued. "Her sister was engaged to be married, to a swell fellow who was a popular high school hero. Gladys knew that another woman had always been in love with her sister's fiance and was jealous of Pat. The other woman was in the car the day Pat died. See this? The date is here on the license plate. 101557. October 15, 1957. That's the date Pat died. The woman hit Pat on the head with something and killed her. Then she pushed the car over the cliff to make it look like accidental death. Somehow Gladys saw it all.

"We'll never know how Gladys knew because Gladys is dead. But it doesn't matter. Gladys told us in the quilt—you are the other woman in the car with Pat!"

The crowd, quiet until now, gasped.

"You saw the quilt sometime in the afternoon, and understood what it meant. You left the Quilt Show on Wednesday evening and went to Gladys' house to confront her. She let you in. You probably argued. You picked up a pair of shears and stabbed her!" Judy made a slashing motion with her hand.

"You took away her drawings of the quilt and then you returned to the Quilt Show and hid the quilt, hoping to keep it out of public view."

The woman had been standing defiantly looking at Judy.

"It's not true. It's all circumstantial. That woman in the quilt could be anyone. You can't prove any of that!" she taunted.

"Yes, I can. You see, the man in the quilt, Pat's fiance, was Tom Lansdowne!"

The crowd that had gathered in a semi–circle and had been standing in a rapt silence listening to Judy, suddenly erupted in a buzz of surprised whispers.

"Somehow he figured out what the quilt meant. He mentioned to us at the show on Thursday that when he first saw the quilt during the judging, he was troubled by it. It seemed familiar to him. He thought he had simply seen it before in another show. But this was the first time this quilt had ever been on display. He probably then found out that the quilt had been made by Gladys, his dead fiancee's little sister, all grown up. Somehow he put it all together and went over to your house to confront you on Friday night..."

The woman interrupted nervously. "He was never at my house!"

"Yes, he was. And what he found made things worse. He found the photo that you have displayed in a shrine you built in his honor. Perhaps he saw it by accident. He was probably appalled by what he saw. You know he saw it, because he dropped his lighter as he left. It's a special lighter, used by pipe–smokers, and it was engraved with his initials. You found it, and you realized that he knew your secret."

"No! No!" She continued to deny the allegations, shaking her head.

"In fact, you've always been in love with him, haven't you? You keep the yearbook open to the page where you and he were photographed together for the Homecoming Ball. You kept the corsage he gave you. You were, in fact, obsessed with him." Judy kept pushing Candice to the edge.

"It's not true..."

"You thought when you removed Pat from the picture forty years ago, he would come to you, but he didn't. He left town and went to California and never came back to Clareville until this weekend. You thought you had a chance to get him back. But he spurned you. He found your silly little shrine and he was shocked, probably sickened!"

"No, he didn't!"

"Yes, he did! I have his fingerprint clear as daylight on the framed photograph that sits on your dresser." Judy pulled another photo from the envelope and shoved it at her. "He left you again, didn't he?"

"So what!" she shrieked, trembling now. "So, he came over for a drink! So what!"

"So when he spurned you, you followed him back to his hotel.

He stopped for gas on the way back—the gas bar in your neighborhood. We found a receipt that has a date and time stamp on it. So you were able to get to the hotel before him. When he came back he ordered room service, and before room service got there you knocked on the door. He let you in. You argued. He threatened to call the police. And then you picked up a golf club and hit him. And you dropped the golf club, right where we found it, in the stairwell. You couldn't remember what had happened to the club, could you?

"He knew that you had killed his fiancee forty years ago. He was furious! Wasn't he? He despised you. He was never going to be yours. Ever!" Judy pushed her face into Candice's and taunted her. "You loved him. And he... hated... you!"

"No. No!" she screamed. "He could never hate me! I loved him so. I loved him so." She began to cry, sobbing into her hands. "He was going to tell the police," she whimpered. "He didn't have to do that. I told him. I would make everything alright. He went to the telephone. I had to stop him. I just wanted to stop him. I would never hurt Tom. I told him I would make everything alright."

Judy straightened up and stook back a pace. The crowd had fallen silent again, waiting for the final, fatal words.

"Candice Moore, I arrest you for the murders of Gladys Brock and Tom Lansdowne. You have the right to remain silent..."

Twelve

The Fifteenth Biannual Clareville Quilt Show is closed.

Black night has folded in with a clear cold October sky. There are no clouds to obscure the deep red Harvest moon as it rises slowly and arcs through the heavens, shrinking and fading to pale yellow. The outrageously flamboyant orb appeared like a gaudy neon sign and now wanes away like a whisper.

Usually when a quilt show finally closes, within seconds the quilts begin to drop from the displays and packing cases litter the aisles as everyone speeds into action dismantling the show. But this time, in Clareville, it took an extra hour for the excitement to calm down at the Quilt Show before anyone was ready to pack up and leave. Four days of conjecture and rumor had finally turned into conclusion and result. The details had to be filled in and reviewed, and exclaimed over. In the end, however, life goes on and everyone had homes to go to, families to spread the news to.

The local business owners are already home and dry. The gypsy vendors have left town for their next destination.

The quilt hanging crew returned to dismantle the displays. The quilts are packed away ready to be picked up or shipped back to their owners. The Hoffman Challenge will travel on to another show. The committee has toted up its gains and losses. Everyone has gone home exhausted, too numb from the excitement of the show and the mystery to think anymore.

The quilters came and saw, were inspired and challenged, shared their love of quilting, and went home satisfied. No one would soon forget this show.

The raffle quilt was won by a man from Syracuse, probably a stranger to town on vacation with his wife who is undoubtedly a quilter. They happened to notice the Quilt Show in The Banner and she dragged him to the show. They will be notified by mail and will be delightfully surprised to receive their treasure by special delivery. They may never know the story behind the Quilt Show where they won the quilt. It's just as well.

The banquet hall is forlornly empty. Except for the pipe–and–drape framing. The commercial display company will come in the morning to dismantle it and the last vestiges of the Show will disappear when the cleaning staff vacuum the carpet. The hall is still and quiet. Yet the lingering echoes of laughter and color remain, haunting the hollow void like the ghosts of friendly quilters past. John has turned off the lights and locked the doors. He's quietly reading another novel in his small closet of an office. His nights will never be quite as peaceful as they were before.

Downtown on the old town square, at The Banner office, Brad is burning the midnight oil on the big story that will break in tomorrow's paper. For once, he has a story that he knows will get picked up on the wire service. For once, he will be sending, not receiving, on the information highway. Luther's in his darkroom alone, working overtime.

Around the corner, Judy is having a quiet dinner at Ivy's restaurant. Sunday is potroast day, and since she can't be bothered to cook a whole roast for one, she ends up here.

"Besides, what would I do with the leftovers?" she shrugged.

"You could get a dog," Ivy suggested, leaning over the back of the benchseat facing Judy, tea towel in hand. "Like Roof," she nodded toward the dog lying at Judy's feet.

"I don't need a dog," Judy laughed. "I have Junior here." She pointed her fork across the table at Jeremy. "He still needs house breaking."

Jeremy went red and bristled defensively.

"Lighten up, kid," Judy leaned forward and punched his arm. "You're alright."

Kitty–corner across the square, the lights are still on in Grama's Quilt Shop. Susan and her mother had unloaded all the boxes and displays from the Show and had put everything back into inventory, ready to open business–as–usual tomorrow morning.

Judy paid her dinner bill and waved goodbye to Ivy as she put on her police cap at the door. She and Jeremy stepped out into the cold night air. She took a deep satisfied breath and exhaled a puff of white steam. Looking across the square she noticed the shop lights on.

"I'll see you tomorrow," she said to Jeremy who was heading toward his squad car. He waved back. There would be plenty of paperwork for both of them Monday morning. In the meantime she could savor her victory.

Judy fastened her jacket and put her hands into her pockets. She hummed 'I Am Woman' happily as she walked across the square, rustling through the fallen leaves. She tapped on the window and Angela let her in.

"Hi," she said smiling cheerfully. "I saw your lights on. Mind if I come in?"

"Not at all, Judy. We were just going to have a cup of chocolate. Would you like one?" Angela offered.

"That would be great! Thanks," Judy said as she unbuttoned her jacket and took off her cap, rubbing her hands. "Cold tonight," she smiled, embarrassed now that she had invited herself in. She wasn't quite sure what she should do now. She looked around at the rainbow shelves full of bolts of fabric. Whew, she thought, all this to make quilts?

"Hi! You can sit here," said Susan, wiggling the stool beside her with her foot.

"Thanks for your help," Judy said as she sat down. She nodded to Susan who then looked puzzled. "The photos, you know," Judy explained.

"Oh, right!" Susan nodded. "Glad to help!"

"I hope you're not investigating another murder," Angela joked as she brought a steaming mug over to Judy.

"No. I...well, actually, I thought the quilts in the Show were really interesting. The ones I got to see. I thought about some of the things you told me about quilting, and I thought I'd like to find out more about it"

"Oh, great. Well, you came to the right place. But you have to watch out for quilters, you know. We're a lot like drug pushers," Angela smiled.

"How's that?" Judy asked in surprise.

"We're always looking to hook in a new quilter and get them addicted!"

Judy laughed. These are really nice women, she thought. I'd like to get to know some of them better. Besides, maybe I'll need a quilt to keep me warm in my old age! I can think of worse fates than that, she decided contentedly.

As she sat at the cutting table with her legs wrapped around the legs of the stool sipping her cocoa, she was facing the shelves of fabric. Several more bolts lay on the cutting table. She picked up one that especially attracted her eye and automatically fingered the material. It was a bold Hoffman print in strong colors.

"This is nice," she commented.

Without saying anything, Susan leaned over and flipped the bolt several times, unfolding a large section of fabric that cascaded over the table. Susan then propped her head on her hand and watched Judy's face for her reaction. A softness and a wistful longing came over Judy's expression as her eyes travelled over the pattern, appreciating the rich design. She was hooked, Susan could see. True quilters have to be able to fall in love with fabric. A true quilter has to be able to surrender herself to the sweet bonds of submission, to the tyrany of color, texture and imagination.

Judy ran her hand over the cloth. She could imagine it would make up into an attractive quilt.

"*Really* nice," Judy repeated and then smiled shyly. Susan smiled.

"If someone was going to start a, um, *stash*, how much fabric would you need?" she asked.

"All depends," Susan shrugged, "on how much you like the fabric. A yard would be plenty. If you were going to mix it with some other fabrics as well..."

Judy laughed. "Well, it looks like I better start somewhere! How about I take a yard of this fabric. And can I sign up for one of your beginner classes?"

"Sure," said Angela, reaching for her scissors.

Susan was about to ring in the sale and her Mom reached over took the piece of fabric, folded it neatly and gave it to Judy. "On the house," she said and waved away Judy's money.

"Are you sure? That's very kind of you. Thank you," Judy was touched by the sudden generosity and happily tucked her treasure into her jacket pocket.

Just then a bustling clatter from the back door signalled Jennifer's return home from her weekend conference. Struggling through the shop door with her bags, she was bright–eyed and excited with all her news. It had been an incredible weekend. She was on cloud nine. She hugged Susan and Angela hello and then noticed the stranger.

"Hi," she said, quizzically.

"Jennifer, this is Deputy Sheriff Judy Marshall. Judy, this is my other daughter, Jennifer."

"Deputy? Have we done something wrong?" Jennifer asked in alarm.

"No, dear. We're just having a cocoa and talking about quilting," Angela explained.

"Right! How was the Quilt Show?" she asked.

"Well, let's see. Can I do this in two hundred words or less?" Angela replied looking at Judy who smiled with amusement. "First Gladys Brock won the Best of Show ribbon. Then her quilt was stolen. Then she was murdered—stabbed with a pair of shears. And the quilt turned up again, hidden in an antique steamer trunk. One of the judges disappeared, and then he was found murdered—hit with a golf club. And it turns out, Candice Moore did it all."

"Yeah right, Mom," Jennifer sarcastically waved off the outlandish description.

"It's true," Susan insisted.

Jennifer looked back and forth at her mother and sister who both nodded. Then she looked at the police woman. Judy nodded.

"No way!" Jennifer sat down stunned. It took several minutes to convince her.

As the three women filled her in on the details, her jaw dropped open further and further.

"This is incredible. This all happened when I was gone for just four days!"

"Yeah," said Susan. "That's the trouble with Clareville. Nothing *Gothic* ever happens here!"